Courteous, courageous and commanding—
these heroes lay it all on the line for the
people they love in more than fifty stories about
loyalty, bravery and romance.
Don't miss a single one!

MEN
in
UNIFORM

USA TODAY Bestselling Author

REBECCA YORK

THE MAN FROM TEXAS

HARLEQUIN®

TORONTO • NEW YORK • LONDON
AMSTERDAM • PARIS • SYDNEY • HAMBURG
STOCKHOLM • ATHENS • TOKYO • MILAN • MADRID
PRAGUE • WARSAW • BUDAPEST • AUCKLAND

ISBN-13: 978-0-373-36254-7

THE MAN FROM TEXAS

Copyright © 2001 by Ruth Glick

REBECCA YORK

Award-winning, bestselling novelist Ruth Glick, who writes as Rebecca York, is the author of more than one hundred books, including her popular 43 Light Street series for Harlequin Intrigue. Ruth says she has the best job in the world. Not only does she get paid for telling stories, she's also the author of twelve cookbooks. Ruth and her husband, Norman, travel frequently, researching locales for her novels and searching out new dishes for her cookbooks.

CHAPTER ONE

It was an indecent hour of the evening, at least as far as Hannah Dawson was concerned. Too early for sleep. And too late to save her immortal soul.

The Baltimore Police Department had assured her that her soul was in no danger. Their seal of approval didn't change her feelings, though—not when eternal truths had been reduced to fuzzy concepts with no weight or substance. All she knew was that it was four months ago to the day that Sean Naylor had died.

So she sat in the Last Chance Bar, nursing the evening's second glass of white wine and wishing she could drown her guilt in drink. The problem was, she hated the effects of alcohol on her brain, which meant she never got very far in the drowning process.

She should go home, she told herself. But she knew the minute she stepped inside her Federal Hill apartment, the walls would start closing in. Leaning back in her chair, she pretended deep interest in her wine while she cataloged the other patrons, as if she were mentally getting ready to stick them in a lineup.

She'd given many of them pet names. Straw Flower, the woman with the dry blond hair who left with a different guy every evening. Paperback Reader, the man who downed three quick shots of bourbon then sat in a corner pretending to read a paperback novel. Suffering Sam, who sat hunched over one drink all evening.

And the new guy. The Outlaw. He'd been here for the past three nights, his rangy body slouched behind a table as he slowly sipped a beer.

He looked out of place in the bar. Out of place in an East Coast city like Baltimore, actually. Riding the range on a horse was more his milieu—with a posse in hot pursuit. Not because he was wearing Western clothing. In fact, his brilliant white running shoes, stiff jeans and inky-black T-shirt looked as if they'd just come off the rack. No, it was the weathered, sunburned look of his face, the way he moved, and the hard muscles of his chest that suggested he'd spent his time outside. And something about his watchful eyes made her think he could be on the run.

From the law?

Or was he, like her, running from himself?

Hannah had noticed him right away and passed a good deal of time covertly studying him. His hair and eyes were dark. His cheekbones sharp. His nose and lips narrow. The face was the kind that would blend well into a crowd. But the easy grace of his movements drew the eyes. At least her eyes.

What kind of voice would go with that hard exterior? More than once she'd imagined herself asking him a question just for the pleasure of hearing the answer. But she never did, of course.

She had the feeling he was giving her a similar once-over, although she'd never actually caught him looking directly at her.

Or perhaps she was making it all up, since the obsession was a way to pass the time, and passing time was one of her chief occupations these evenings.

She glanced at her watch. Eleven-thirty. Too early to go home. Too late to stanch the restless feeling in her gut.

After paying for her drinks, she exited into the night, aware of the reassuring weight of her Sig Sauer in its holster under her jacket. This wasn't the worst neighborhood in the city, but she'd learned caution from her days in the Baltimore P.D. Of course, she didn't know whether she'd lost the ability to fire the gun at another human being. She'd have to face that obstacle when she came to it.

She sucked in several breaths of the cool spring night air, then started toward the row house where she'd rented a room for the past few years. As a Baltimore City cop, she'd liked living close to her work. Now that she'd resigned from the force, she'd lost some of her enthusiasm for the city, but she still found the location convenient to her new job at the Light Street Detective Agency.

Out on the streets, old habits asserted themselves. When Hannah thought she heard footsteps behind her, she stopped and surveyed the area. But a man only walked past, moving rapidly down the block and disappearing inside a row house.

She passed her own apartment and kept going toward the Science Center. Pulling the collar of her jacket closed, she stood for a few minutes watching the lights of the shopping pavilions winking at her across the water of the refurbished Inner Harbor, wondering what it would be like to step into a time machine and repeat the last six months of her life. Would she do anything differently? Or had her fate been sealed when she'd been assigned to the Turner investigation?

Her hands clenched as she remembered the tongue-lashing she'd gotten from Gary Flynn, the man she'd thought she loved.

"Suck it up and get over it, Troop. If you don't want to

shoot bad guys, quit and go to work at Burger King. Then you can have it your way. Until then, stop whining and get your ass back out on the street where it belongs."

There had been more. Worse. Things she'd never thought she'd hear from someone who cared about her. She'd stared at him in shock, stood with her arms wrapped protectively around her shoulders as he'd walked away with a disgusted expression on his face.

As soon as he'd left the room, her knees had buckled and she'd sunk into a chair by the window. The next morning, she'd mustered the strength to pack her clothes and leave. And after a couple of nights in the spare room of her friends Jessie and Miguel Valero, she'd found her own apartment.

She'd salved her pride a little with the knowledge that she was the one who'd moved out. But that hadn't eased any of the pain.

All at once it was impossible to stop her mind from spinning back to the worst moments of her life. Four months ago to the day.

She was on another darkened street—this one strewn with trash. She and two other police detectives, facing a group of tough-looking drug dealers.

One of them hurled an obscenity into the darkness. Another drew a gun and fired, the noise reverberating in her head. Then her own gun was in her hand, and she was squeezing the trigger—once, twice.

Around her, the night air exploded with sound. Gunshots. Running feet. Shouts of fear. When the crisis was over, one of the drug dealers lay on the sidewalk gasping for breath, the front of his shirt covered with blood. When Hannah knelt beside him, he turned his face toward her, made a gurgling sound in his throat, called for his mother.

As she stared down into his cloudy eyes, all she could think was that he looked like a scared, confused kid who'd sneaked out of the house when his parents thought he was home in bed.

The sound of an ambulance filled her brain. Then paramedics pushed her out of the way, working over the limp body on the sidewalk.

She hadn't known then whether it had been a bullet from her gun that had killed Sean Naylor. Later, she'd found out that it wasn't. But that hadn't done anything to ease her guilt.

The memory was so vivid, the awful feelings so strong that the awareness of her surroundings had completely faded from her consciousness. But the present snapped back into focus with vivid clarity as she felt a body hurtle out of the darkness, crashing against her with enough force to knock her off her feet. She had time for only a choked scream as a large male shape took her down to the cold pavement, covered her body with his.

God, how could she be so stupid? On the street at night and oblivious.

"Got ya, bitch," a voice snarled as the back of her head collided with the edge of the pavement. Momentarily paralyzed from the blow, she felt steely fingers close around her throat, shutting off her oxygen supply. Her hand scrabbled desperately for her gun, but a knee pinned her arm in place, and the hands clamped around her windpipe made her feel as though time and space were contracting around her.

Her hearing faded, her vision blurred and her limbs turned to lead. Then, just before she blacked out completely, the body covering hers was suddenly ripped away, and sounds came toward her from out of the darkness. Swinging her eyes to the right, she saw two men fighting, rolling across the ground, trading punches. There was a grunt, a shout and then what looked like a desperate struggle for freedom on the part of one of the combatants. He tore himself loose and dashed away into the night.

Still gasping for breath, she watched as the other man pushed himself up and tore off after the running figure.

In a few minutes one of the men was back, cursing as he knelt on the pavement and loomed over her. Hannah didn't even know which one he was—her attacker or her savior. Before she could make another try for her gun, he grabbed her hand in a grip that immobilized her whole arm. But his voice was as smooth as aged bourbon as he drawled, "It's okay. I'm not going to hurt you."

He shifted so that light from the harbor illuminated his chiseled features, and she saw it was the man from the bar. The one she'd called the Outlaw.

It was difficult to make her eyes focus on him. Difficult to put any strength into her voice. But she managed the latter. "What are you doing here?"

"I was following you," he answered, as if that was all the explanation she needed, would ever need.

"Why?"

"I saw a guy fall into step behind you when you walked out the door."

So she'd been right in the first place about being followed, her dazed brain informed her—for all the good it had done her. She'd been too caught up in the past to keep her mind on her surroundings. Stupid. Very stupid.

"You're hurt," he said, and it registered in her solar plexus that his voice was a perfect foil for his tough exterior. Low and husky and slow, with a nice touch of down-home warmth.

His hands moved up and down her arms, then her legs, his touch much too intimate.

When she slapped at his hand, he shook his head. "Don't. I'm just makin' sure you don't have any broken bones."

"I'm all right," she answered too quickly. As she pushed herself up, she felt a sharp pain several inches above the place where her head joined her neck. To her vast relief it settled into a dull throb.

"What is it? Your head?"

"Umm."

He looked up and down the street before his attention turned back to her. "You need to get inside, darlin'."

Rock-solid arms lifted her to her feet. She wanted to tell him that she didn't need any help. But protest had moved beyond her reach. So she directed him down the sidewalk in the direction from which she'd come, to the converted row house where she lived, and up a flight of steps to number three.

When she simply stood there in the hallway, swaying like a flower in a light breeze, he reached into her right front pocket, his fingers groping her thigh.

Hannah roused herself enough to demand, "What the hell do you think you're doing now?"

"Gettin' your key. Gettin' you out of harm's way," he answered, his tone going gruff.

He pulled the key from her pocket, inserted it in the lock and turned.

He was still holding her with one hand as he pushed the door open. Wrenching away, she careened across the threshold and into the living room, landing heavily in the easy chair beside the old mantelpiece.

The effort had winded her, and she slumped there, breathing in painful gasps.

He stood where he was, his hands shoved into his pockets,

as if he knew damn well that she wouldn't welcome any more physical contact. Still, his assessment from four feet away was unnerving.

Trying to ignore him, Hannah reached to cup the back of her throbbing head and encountered sticky wetness. When she brought her hand down to eye level, she saw that her palm was red with blood.

Her gasp brought him instantly to her side. When he saw the blood, he gave her a reassuring look. "Head wounds tend to bleed like a son of a bitch, but I'd better wash it off and see what's going on."

She wanted to tell him she didn't need any help. Instead, she simply sat there, too lethargic to protest when he disappeared down the hall. All she could do was lean forward to keep the blood from getting on the corduroy slipcover she'd sent to the cleaners when she'd been in her demon-housekeeper phase.

A few moments later, he reappeared with a hand towel, some antiseptic and a box of gauze pads from her medicine cabinet. Standing beside the chair, he cradled her head against his taut middle with one hand, and she closed her eyes, taking slow deep breaths and trying not to react to the physical contact.

She had been numb inside for a long time, and now, as this stranger held her head and moved his fingers gently through her hair, she felt something inside herself stir—something she didn't welcome.

Not after what had happened with Gary. A long time ago he'd held her with the same tenderness, undressed her, washing her shoulder where she'd been hit by flying glass. And she'd thought she could depend on his comfort and support for the rest of her life. That was only a few months before she'd found out how things really stood between them.

The memory made her stiffen. When she tried to jerk away from the man who cradled her head, his hold tightened—not painfully but with a commanding firmness.

"Easy, darlin'," he said in the slow, delicious voice that started to melt the frozen block of ice deep inside her.

She felt his stomach muscles ripple as he pressed her cheek more tightly to his body, but he said nothing more as he brushed aside her hair and carefully swabbed the raw wound on her scalp with antiseptic.

"You've got a knot back here, and a cut. Not too deep. But it could use a couple of stitches."

"No."

"What do you mean no?"

Damned if she was going to let anyone know she'd messed up this evening. A picture flashed in her mind: her in the emergency room, bumping into some of her former colleagues on the police force who were there on official business. They'd be surprised and sympathetic. They'd ask what had happened to her. Then next thing you knew, everyone would be talking about how she'd screwed up.

The Outlaw held her head in his large hand, tipping her face up to his, and she was swallowed by the dark pools of his eyes. "Darlin', you're not making sense."

She knew he was right. She wasn't making sense. Not on any kind of rational level. But there was no way she was going to bare her feelings to him.

She didn't know what he saw in her eyes at that moment. Determination? Fear? Hostility? Whatever it was, he dropped his hands away from her and took a step back.

"That cut needs attention," he said. "I'd vote for stitches. But I can try a butterfly bandage. The scar will be bigger, but I guess it won't matter much under that gorgeous hair."

Somewhere in her mind the personal comment registered. But she was too relieved by his acquiescence to call him on it. Instead, she answered, "Okay," hating the feeling of relief that swept over her.

He wheeled, strode down the hall again and returned almost at once with adhesive tape and scissors.

"You seem to know your way around my apartment pretty well," she muttered as he tore off a strip of tape and started cutting it into a butterfly shape.

"Because you're as organized as an old-lady librarian. Everything's in its logical place."

She wasn't sure she liked that image. Since childhood, orderliness had been her defense against the uncertainties of the world around her. But before she had time to think about it, he turned her mind to other things—like his formidable physical presence. Moving in close again, he tipped her head down and pressed the towel against the wound.

"Sorry, I've got to cut a little patch of your hair," he said.

She nodded, conscious of her face resting against his taut middle. She dragged in a breath and drew in his scent—a combination of no-nonsense soap and masculinity.

Although she couldn't see what he was doing, Hannah sensed he was working with speed and economy. Deftly he snipped away some of her hair, then applied the butterfly strip of adhesive, and taped a gauze pad over top.

"Where did you learn all that first-aid stuff?" she asked as he stepped back and began gathering up the materials he'd left on the table beside the chair.

His hands stopped. "Around," he said in a slow, countrified voice that made her wonder if he'd picked up his doctoring abilities in a farmyard. Before she could evaluate his reaction, he swept everything into the towel and whirled away.

She raised her hand to the small bandage on the back of her head, gingerly feeling the knot beneath the gauze as she watched his broad shoulders disappear into the bathroom, heard him replacing supplies on the shelves of the medicine cabinet.

It was time to take charge of the situation, she thought, slipping her right hand down to the holster at her hip.

When her uninvited guest came back down the hall, he had a flashlight in his hand. "I'm going to check your pupils," he said in response to her questioning look.

She nodded, winced, then winced again as he directed the beam at her face. "Well?" she managed to say.

He took a step back. "They're contracting okay. But are you sure you don't want to go to the emergency room?"

"Absolutely sure," she retorted. "I'm fine."

"Are you? You let somebody get the drop on you tonight. Now you're giving a perfect stranger the run of your apartment."

"Not exactly." The hand that she'd hidden between her hip and the side of the chair emerged, holding her Sig Sauer. She concentrated on keeping the gun steady—and keeping her features firm. No point in letting him know that she hadn't used a gun anywhere but a firing range since she'd left the department.

LUKE'S EYES zeroed in on the gun, and he made a split-second decision. He'd known as soon as he helped her up that she was armed. And he'd been sure that he could take the weapon away from her with very little effort. But if it made her more comfortable to think she'd gotten the drop on him, fine.

Slowly he raised his hands to shoulder level and tried to convey a sense of calm compliance. "I'm going to take a couple steps back and sit on the sofa. Is that okay?"

When she nodded, he backed up and sat down carefully. No sudden moves.

"You don't have to keep that thing pointed at me. If I wanted to wallop you, I'd have done it already," he pointed out.

"Is that supposed to be reassuring?" Still, she lowered the weapon as she studied him.

He returned the scrutiny with a level gaze, silently reaffirming his judgment that he'd picked the right woman for the job he had in mind. She was tough. Cautious. And, despite tonight's nasty little incident, capable of defending herself.

She interrupted his thoughts with a pointed question. "Okay, you said you saw a guy follow me out of the bar. How come you got involved?"

"I'm the white-knight type."

"You could have fooled me."

"Meaning?"

"Meaning, you look like a guy on the run."

His shoulder lifted in a small shrug.

"I want some straight answers from you," she said. "You've been scoping me out for a couple of nights now. Then you followed me out of the bar. I want to know what's going on."

He worked to keep the corners of his lips from twitching. With her dander up, she was cute as a button. But he owed her an explanation. Sobering, he said, "Okay, I want to hire your services as a private detective."

She stared at him as if she hadn't heard him right. "You want to hire the services of a bumbling idiot who lets herself get assaulted in the street, then lets a strange guy into her apartment."

"Don't forget, you neutralized him with your gun," he answered.

"The way you say it, I get the feeling you're not too worried."

He waved his hand dismissively, then turned the focus of

the discussion away from himself and back to her. "This evening's about as typical for you as a hound dog singing opera. You've got an excellent record as a cop. And you've joined the city's premier private investigation firm, the Light Street Detective Agency. Formerly O'Malley and Lancer. But Jo O'Malley has gone on leave. And Mike Lancer is planning to move to his wife's hometown in Pennsylvania. So after interviewing dozens of candidates, the agency has taken on two new detectives—you and Sam Lassiter."

She peered at him quizzically. "It sounds like you've been checking up on me."

"I'd be a dang fool to hire you unless I'd done my homework."

"And what exactly do you want me to do for you? I don't even know your name."

He gave a harsh laugh. "That's exactly the problem. I want you to find out who I am."

He watched her big hazel eyes blink rapidly a couple times. Probably she was wondering if she'd heard him right. In point of fact, he was wondering how he'd gotten the words out of his own mouth.

But the time had come to put up or shut up. And he chose the former.

"I want you to discover my identity," he clarified.

"You don't know who you are? You're saying you have amnesia?"

"Jackpot."

"Have you been to the police? The FBI?"

"Not a good idea."

While she waited for clarification, he let out a small sigh. He'd convinced himself he could trust her. Now that the time had come, he felt like a cat clinging to a tin roof by its claws.

"Three weeks ago I woke up in a hotel room in Chicago. Before that I don't remember a blasted thing."

Her eyes widened. "You have no memories before that?"

"That's right."

"So how did you end up in Baltimore?"

He'd tried to answer that question a number of times. Now he gave her the line that he'd given himself. "It was just another place. A city big enough to hide in. And not so spread out that it's hard to get around."

"You're sure that's all?"

He swallowed. "Okay. Something—a feeling—drew me here. I can't tell you any more than that."

He watched her, knowing she was trying to decide whether to press the subject or drop it. Finally, she raised her hand to her face, and he followed the movement of her graceful fingers as she massaged her temple.

"Your head hurts," he said, snatching at the excuse to postpone the inevitable. "This isn't a good time to get into a bunch of stuff."

"We're already into a bunch of stuff."

"Yeah. But I think you should get some sleep, and we should continue the conversation in the morning."

She shook her head, grimaced. "Stop dancing around, and tell me flat out why you don't want to do what any normal amnesia victim would do."

He sucked in a deep breath and let it out slowly, wishing he hadn't lost control of the situation. But he knew from his research that she was good at mining for information—making things go her way, even when she was obviously in pain.

"Okay. I told you I woke up in a Chicago hotel room. I had a knot on my head—a lot worse than the one you've got. And I had two suitcases with me. One was full of new clothing I have no memory of buying. The other—" He stopped and swallowed before he was able to continue. "The other was full of money. Damn near a million dollars."

CHAPTER TWO

He watched her jaw drop, part of him amused by the classic reaction. "You're kidding me."

"Darlin', I wish I were."

"Where did the money come from?"

He shrugged. "I've got some theories." When she didn't comment, he was forced to continue. "It's got to be from some shady deal—a drug payoff, blackmail money, something like that."

The words hung between them.

"Not necessarily," she finally said. "Maybe you're a courier who thwarted a robbery attempt and were injured in the process."

"A courier for whom?"

"I don't know."

"And you're in no shape to think about it now. We should have started this discussion in the morning. You need to sleep. I'll stay here in case you get into trouble."

"You're telling me you think you're a criminal, and you're staying in my apartment? I don't think so."

He spread his hands, palms up. "I'm doing what's best for you, considering that you won't go to the emergency room."

"You don't remember your name, but you know what's best for *me*."

"I'm using common sense."

"Uh-huh. And what name are you using, by the way?"

"Luke Pritchard."

"Where'd you come up with that?"

"I let my fingers do the walkin' through a phone book," he said with a shrug of his shoulders. "One from column A and one from column B."

"There's no significance to the combination?"

"I just liked the way it sounded," he answered, aware again of that little twinge of reaction. Luke Pritchard meant something. But he was damned if he could figure out what.

He watched her take in his uncertain expression.

"You're right. We can continue the discussion in the morning. Come back at…eight."

"Okay," he agreed, because it was easier than arguing.

Demonstrating his spirit of cooperation, he climbed off the sofa and strode to the front door. After stepping into the hall and closing the door, he listened to the sound of her snapping the dead bolt into place.

She was cautious. Which was good. But he'd bet she was in no shape to check the lock he'd opened on the bathroom window.

At the bottom of the stairs he paused, his long-fingered hand clutching the door frame. Deliberately, he eased the pressure of his fingers, even while he questioned his own judgment. He'd picked over Hannah Dawson's background like a sheep farmer combing burrs out of a ewe's coat—and assured himself that she was the right person to help him.

Right now, he knew her better than any other human being on earth. He knew she was from York, Pennsylvania. Knew that her father had been a truck driver and that her mom had worked in a school cafeteria. He knew the parents were both dead—the father of lung cancer and the mother of a heart attack. She was the youngest of four siblings, ten years younger than her closest brother; a baby who had come late in her parents' lives. She was the only one who had gone to college, and on a scholarship. The others had resented her advancing in the world, so she rarely communicated with them.

Her uncle, also deceased, had been a police officer in town. She'd admired him and been inspired to follow in his footsteps. But apparently, sticking around York hadn't been an option for her, so she'd applied to the Baltimore P.D. out of college.

Luke knew she'd been determined to make something of herself. Determined to be the best detective in the department. He knew all the facts. But in the end, the facts hadn't been the deciding factor. He'd picked her based on emotion, not logic. He was attracted to her, and now that he'd spent some time with her, he knew the attraction was dangerous.

He stood in the doorway, picturing the woman who'd locked him out of her apartment with such a decisive snick of her dead bolt. Her wide hazel eyes had looked so gentle—until you got her dander up. Then there was the sable hair cropped at chin level. As he'd covertly studied her in the Last Chance Bar, he'd wondered about the texture. Now he knew it was soft and silky to the touch. Like her creamy skin. Probably her pretty little lips were soft as well.

He found himself getting turned on thinking about how those lips would feel brushing against his, opening under his. In some part of his brain he knew he should run—not walk—back to his temporary town house. But he remained where he was, because the terrible feeling of isolation, of loneliness, wouldn't allow him to leave.

He had no memories of mother, father, sisters, brothers, friends…wife. Holding up his left hand, he inspected his ring finger as he had so many times over the past few weeks. It was bare. And there was no indentation or circle of lighter skin where a ring might have been. But that proved nothing, of course. For all he knew, he could have a wife and children stashed in Anchorage, Alaska, or right here in Baltimore.

If he did, he recalled nothing about them. Or anyone else who might have meant something to him personally. Or himself, for that matter.

He pressed his fingertips against the skin of his face, feeling the rough texture. He'd spent a great deal of his life outside. Maybe he was a telephone lineman—who'd gotten an electric shock from the wires at the top of the pole, lost his memory and stumbled over a suitcase full of money.

He made a snorting sound. The lineman theory made as little sense as any of the other nut-brained scenarios he'd manufactured over the past weeks as he'd lain in bed with his hands stacked behind his head—sleepless in Chicago, Denver, St. Louis, Baltimore.

Once again he went over the things he knew, hoping they would trigger some memory.

He was strong. He had the reflexes of a cat burglar.

He stopped there—picturing himself dressed in black quietly treading across a roof at night. It wasn't hard to make the image seem real. In a few minutes, he was going to make it real, but he didn't know whether it was an actual memory.

He was good with a gun. An automatic felt familiar in his hand. He knew how many bullets there were in the magazine of a Sig Sauer P-228. He knew how to sight and fire, how to clean and maintain a weapon.

So, was he on the right side of the law or the wrong? He had the instincts of a fugitive; he knew that much. He had to assume somebody was looking for him and the money, but he'd successfully evaded them by buying a false identity, maintaining a low profile and keeping his nose clean.

Another thing he knew was that his mind was sharp. He had excellent reasoning, a lot of specific facts at his fingertips and broad general knowledge. But anything pertaining specifically to himself was locked away behind a metaphorical eight-foot stone wall topped with razor wire.

His hands squeezed in frustration. Then he roused himself, strode down the block and found the alley running along the back of the row houses. He'd been here before, so he knew which unit was Hannah's. He'd also thought about how to get inside if he needed to.

She'd told him she didn't want him in her apartment tonight. But she'd also been attacked an hour ago. And he'd heard the assailant call out, "Got ya, bitch."

Suppose that shout was personal? Suppose the assailant had a grudge to settle with her? If that were true, the guy could come back tonight, which meant that leaving Hannah unguarded was dangerous and irresponsible. So whether or not she wanted him in her apartment tonight, he was fixin' to be there—watching over her.

HANNAH STOOD for a moment listening to the silence around her. The man who'd picked the name Luke Pritchard for himself was gone, and the apartment felt strangely empty.

Like everything else in her life. She'd come to Baltimore with such hope, determined to be as good a cop as her uncle Jacob had been. And for a few years, she'd thought she was living up to the high standard he'd set.

Now her dreams were shattered along with her confidence. She was a washed-up cop holding on to some measure of self-respect by working as a P.I.

In her bedroom, she flicked on the lamp that hung over the bed, and closed the door before setting her gun down on the nightstand with a thunk.

Her eyes darted to the phone beside the gun. Maybe she *should* ask someone to stay with her. A few months ago she wouldn't have had to call anyone. Gary would have been lying beside her in their bed and he would have taken her in his arms as he soothed her.

She squeezed her eyes shut to banish that image. Gary was gone. He wasn't coming back. And one thing she was certain of was that she didn't want him back!

The person to call was Sam Lassiter or one of her other Light Street friends, and they'd be here inside of fifteen minutes. But she wasn't going to make any calls at—she glanced at the clock and was astonished to find it was after one in the morning.

Stripping down to her panties, she pulled on an oversize T-shirt. Then, finding she was swaying on her feet again, she flopped onto the bed and slipped under the covers. It was almost too much effort to turn off the lamp, but she managed.

In the darkness her thoughts turned back to Luke Pritchard, remembering the conversation between them. It had been difficult for him to tell her what he wanted, but finally he'd trusted her with the secret he must have been lugging around like a steamer trunk for three weeks. She remembered the look on his face when he'd told her about the money. A mixture of defiance and sadness and underlying fear that he was struggling to hide. But she'd seen it, and she'd understood, because something similar had happened to her a few months ago. Maybe not in the same way. But she knew what it felt like to have your identity yanked away and to find yourself struggling to figure out who you were. He was doing the same thing, only he had no background, no past experience to help him out.

She shuddered. In the privacy of her bedroom, she was willing to admit that she'd been feeling sorry for herself for months. She'd walked away from a job that had been her life. And her man had as good as slapped her in the face with her own inadequacies.

She winced, then set her jaw. Someone with worse problems than hers had ended up on her doorstep. Someone who needed her.

But she wasn't going to be stupid about trusting him. She hadn't agreed to take the job he was offering. There was still time to back out if she thought that working for the man was too dangerous.

LUKE WAITED in the alley outside Hannah's apartment a full thirty minutes after he saw the bedroom light flick off. Then instead of making a direct assault on her apartment, he started several houses down where a breakfast room had been added to the kitchen. Using the fence to boost himself up, he silently and quickly transferred to the roof of the addition, then hoisted himself to the second-story room, using the drainpipe as a handhold.

Once he was on the roof, he waited for several minutes to make sure there had been no reaction to his presence. As he moved along the row of houses, he wondered if he really *had* been a cat burglar.

At Hannah's he used the fancy blockwork at the side of the building as a ladder, clinging to the rectangular stones as he made his way down to the second level, where he transferred to the bathroom-window ledge, holding himself in place with one hand while he eased open the window with the other.

Again he waited to see if his presence had been noted. When Hannah didn't charge through the door with her gun in her hand, he pushed the window as wide as it would go, freezing when it gave a squeak of protest.

But Hannah still didn't appear. Now came the tricky part, he thought as he maneuvered first one broad shoulder and then the other through the narrow opening. Once his torso was inside, he grasped the window frame and hauled the rest of his body into the bathroom, using his arms to control his headfirst descent to the floor.

Pleased to note that the exertion hadn't particularly winded him, he stood and closed the window. He wiped his hands on a hand towel over the sink.

After removing his shoes, he paused outside the bedroom door. It was difficult to keep himself from easing it open and making sure she was all right. But that would be pushing his luck.

So he made his way down the hall to the living room and dropped into the chair Hannah had sat in earlier.

He was immediately conscious of the scent she'd left behind. Woman and floral shampoo, because he didn't think she was the kind who would bother with perfume. She'd felt so fragile in his arms when he'd helped her back to the apartment. But it was her inner strength that had drawn him to her in the first place.

Eyes closed, he slumped down into the feminine aura, his head cushioned by the chair back and his hands clutching the padded arms. Deliberately, he eased the pressure of his fingers, even while he questioned his own judgment for the second time that evening.

He must be crazy coming in here like this. But he wasn't about to leave, not after all the effort he'd put out.

One thing he'd discovered about himself—he was persistent. Another was that he had the ability to sleep lightly like a cat and wake instantly when necessary. He glanced at his watch. It was almost two in the morning. He'd make sure he was out of the apartment by six at the latest. Then he'd go back to his town house, shower and shave, and come back for the appointment they'd made.

FAR TO THE WEST of Baltimore, in San Diego, a man who called himself Dallas Sedgwick sat in an easy chair contemplating his options.

For the past three weeks he'd had men out beating the bushes for a very cunning fugitive. A man who had stolen a million dollars from him and then disappeared like smoke wafting away on the wind.

There were several problems involved with finding him— the first being that with the amount of cash at his disposal, he could be anywhere in the world by now.

Then there was the question of his identity. Dallas had a picture of the man but no name that would do him any good. He thought about the stupid son of a bitch who had vouched for this viper, Rafael Concha. He would have taken Concha out to a patch of uninhabited desert wasteland, stripped him naked and staked him to the ground on top of a fire-ant hill. But Concha had already died on a godforsaken patch of real estate south of the Rio Grande, so Dallas wouldn't have the pleasure of torturing him until he talked.

Opening the folder that rested on his lap, he got out several photographs of the man who had disappeared with the money. They were all candid shots, some full face, some profile, all snapped after the traitor had come to work for him.

There was nothing remarkable about the fugitive. He had

dark hair and eyes, sharp cheekbones, narrow lips and nose, weathered skin. He'd been hired because he was ruthless, skilled with a gun and knew his way around the desert along the border.

Dallas had been considering giving him a raise. Then he'd gone out with a team and never come back. In fact, nobody had come back. Most of the others were confirmed dead. But no one with the height and weight and coloring of the man in question was among them.

Which meant he and some accomplice had killed the rest of the guys with him. Or he'd been damn lucky to get away from an ambush.

Dallas didn't care which it was. All he wanted was his money back and the man in custody.

Long ago he'd learned what was important in life. Power. Money. Respect. He had absorbed those lessons at his father's knee. Dad had held his sons to a high standard, then pitted them against the one person he might have loved. Another man might have cursed his father for isolating him from his family. Dallas appreciated the values he'd learned. Dad's training had been harsh, but it had made him tough and ruthless, prepared him for the real world. Dallas knew how to make money, how to keep it and how to ensure the loyalty of the men under him. Which meant the man who'd stolen from him and disappeared must be found and punished appropriately.

A tap on the door made him look up, then call out, "Come in."

Chad Crosby, one of his lieutenants, stepped into the room. Despite the early hour of the morning, Crosby was dressed in a crisp blue shirt and navy trousers. "Sorry to disturb you, sir," he said.

"I take it there's been a development."

Crosby held up a cassette box. "This is a tape from a bank surveillance camera in Baltimore. I think you'll find it interesting."

THE LIGHT OUTSIDE had turned gray when a noise from the bedroom woke Luke. A muffled scream. Or perhaps a loud gasp.

His reaction was swift and primal. Propelling himself out of the chair and cursing his lack of a weapon, he sprinted down the hall. As he burst through the bedroom door, he expected to see an assailant attacking Hannah. But she was alone, thrashing around in her double bed. She'd kicked the covers off, and he got a good view of long legs, shapely hips and bikini panties below a white T-shirt that had tangled itself around her waist.

The view was mesmerizing and unsettling at the same time because he knew she was caught in the grip of a nightmare. He also knew how she'd react if she caught him standing there looking at her half-naked body. He should get the hell out of her bedroom. But when she moaned again, he felt as if a giant blade had pierced his chest.

"Hannah."

As he took an uncertain step forward and then another, her eyes snapped open and zeroed in on him.

He was trapped like a bull in a box canyon. And it was his own damn arrogant fault.

He saw her blink, saw her lunge for the gun on the bedside table. This time he knew that letting her get to the weapon first might be a death sentence—for both of them. So he beat her to it, swept the gun out of her grasp and set it down on the dresser behind him.

When she tried to throw herself from the bed, he came down beside her, wrapping his arms around her to keep her from mauling him.

"Get off me, you son of a bitch," she panted, flailing at him with her feet, so that he had to shift his leg on top of hers to thwart her efforts to emasculate him.

"Hannah, don't. Stop it. I'm not going to hurt you. I swear."

The assurance did nothing to ease her tense muscles. "What the hell are you doing in my bedroom?" she demanded.

"You cried out. I thought the guy who tried to strangle you on the sidewalk had gotten in." He repeated the explanation, sighing in relief when she stopped trying to maul him. But he was still hesitant to turn her loose for fear that she was just waiting for her chance to turn the tables. Her head tipped up, and her eyes bored into his. "What exactly are you doing in my apartment after I asked you to leave?"

"Under the circumstances, I thought you shouldn't be left alone."

"So you took it upon yourself to break in?"

He kept his gaze steady. "Yes."

She muttered something that didn't sound very ladylike. "Get off of me."

"If you promise not to knee me in the *cojones*."

She thought about it for several seconds before nodding her agreement.

Flopping to his back, he lay with his shoulder touching hers, emotions roiling inside him. He felt like a damn fool for having gotten into this situation, and at the same time he knew he was perfectly justified in having decided to protect her.

"Get out of here," she whispered, and he suspected that she wasn't capable of talking louder.

His own voice was none too steady as he answered, "Not while you're thinkin' of me like a skunk in the woodpile."

"A skunk in the woodpile. That's a pretty good description. And it's your own damn fault. What in the heck do you think you were doing?"

He ignored her words and the hot, sharp tightness in his chest. "I came down the hall because I thought you were in trouble. Then I saw you were thrashing around on the bed, having a bad dream."

"Oh!" The syllable came out high and choked.

He literally felt her control snap. When he turned toward her, he saw her shoulders begin to shake, and her eyes fill with tears.

"Darlin', don't."

The only effect of his words was to make the tears come harder and faster.

Instinctively he reached for her, gathered her close, amazed once again at how fragile she felt in his arms. For several heartbeats she struggled to free herself as he held her tightly, not the way he had before but with all the tenderness he was feeling.

She gave up the fight, leaning in to him, her shoulders heaving as the misery seized her.

Overwhelmed, he felt her give herself into his care, at least for the moment. He crooned low reassuring words that were as much for himself as for the woman in his arms. Dipping his head, he skimmed his lips against her hair, then pressed his cheek to the top of her head as his own vision blurred, because the feeling of being needed was almost too much for him to cope with.

He held her, caressed her, soothed her, feeling the storm of her emotions build, then begin to ebb. When he sensed that the tears had all been shed, he reached for a tissue on the nightstand and handed it to her.

Ducking her head, she blew her nose.

"Better?"

"Yes."

"Do you remember the dream?" he asked softly.

She remained huddled into herself. Without raising her head, she answered, "I don't want to talk about it. Not to you."

Or anyone else, he suspected.

"You'll feel better if you do."

"How do you know?"

He gave her as much honesty as he could—enough to make his stomach clench. "Because I know how bad it feels to bottle everything up inside yourself when there's no one you can trust."

"You're saying I can trust you?"

"I hope you can."

She kept her face averted, and he felt himself holding his breath, wondering how she was going to respond. Outside, the gray light had brightened, and he could hear birds waking up in the trees.

Finally she said, "The nightmares are the same. It's always about Sean Naylor." She swallowed. "He's the reason I left the Baltimore P.D. Last night was the four-month anniversary of his death."

She paused, and he reached around her, rubbing at the knot of tension at the base of her neck.

When she began to speak again, her voice was flat and dead. "I was assigned to the Turner investigation. They're an organization in Baltimore distributing drugs. We had a tip that a big deal was going down—but we'd been given the wrong time. So we got there just as the participants were arriving. Some of them fled. One of them was killed. Sean Naylor. An eighteen-year-old kid, for Lord's sake."

"You didn't kill him," he said with absolute conviction.

"I could have, although the bullet wasn't from my gun, as it turned out. But I was the one who knelt there on the sidewalk waiting for the paramedics, watching the life ebb out of him."

"You couldn't have done anything."

"I still don't even know if he was in on the deal. It looks like he was with the guys who were, but I can't even be sure of that."

"So you blamed your own judgment and quit the force. But it wasn't simply your judgment. There were other cops involved, one of whom shot the kid."

"I as good as pulled the trigger! Knowing that, I couldn't stay. Not when I realized I was going to hesitate every time I had to pull my weapon. Out on the street, I'd be endangering my own life and that of every cop who worked with me."

He suspected she was putting the trauma into practical terms and skirting the guilt she still felt. But he wasn't going to call her on it.

"So now you know that if you get into a tight spot with me, I may let you down," she said.

"I'm willing to take a chance on you."

"What if I'm not willing to do the same?"

He was instantly sizzling with tension. "What's that supposed to mean?"

Her jaw firmed. "It means that you can climb out of my bed and go out through the front door and find yourself another detective. Because I'm not going to be working with you."

CHAPTER THREE

"No."

"What do you mean no?" Hannah echoed.

"I mean I'm not letting you show me the door. I need you."

Hannah stared at him, and the haunted expression in his dark eyes said that he was telling the truth. He had the desperate look of a man clinging to a rope over a canyon—and the rope was breaking strand by strand.

She saw him swallow. "I was fixin' to leave before you woke up, but I heard you cry out, and I came charging down the hall. Breaking in was a mistake in judgment, and I apologize for that. But I was too worried about you to leave you alone."

His voice had turned stiff, and she wondered how many apologies he'd made in his life. The knowledge that neither one of them had the answer was enough to sway her judgment.

"Okay, you can tell me everything you know about your situation over breakfast. Then I'll decide whether I'm a damn fool to take you on."

She saw him let out the breath he'd been holding.

"Deal. I'll cook while you take a shower." Without giving her a chance to argue, he climbed out of her bed and strode toward the door.

She watched his broad shoulders disappear, wondering

how she could possibly work with a man who made her feel so vulnerable. She hadn't let anyone see her cry over Sean Naylor—not since Gary had told her to get her butt back in gear. But the man who called himself Luke Pritchard had gotten her to open up with very little effort.

Grabbing clean underwear along with a fresh T-shirt and jeans, she ducked into the bathroom and locked the door—and the window. It wasn't until she'd turned on the water that she remembered that her unwanted guest had taped up her scalp the night before. Gingerly she touched the bandage. Probably it wasn't a good idea to get it wet, she thought as she pulled a shower cap from the shelf over the toilet.

While she stood under the hot spray, she thought about everything that had happened over the past few months—and everything that had happened since Luke had come to her aid the night before. Once she'd thought she was a good judge of men. That confidence had been shaken, and now here she was, faced with the decision of trusting another guy.

Well, she'd try to be smart this time. She'd ask him some hard questions. And she wouldn't take the job unless he seemed to be playing it straight with her about his problem.

When she emerged from the bathroom, she was immediately enveloped by the delicious aromas drifting toward her. Following her nose down the hall, she found Luke towering over the stove, looking too large for her small kitchen. Yet he seemed thoroughly at home stirring a skillet with frying onions, peppers and small pieces of bacon.

When she stepped through the doorway he gave her a long inspection. Too long.

"How are you feeling?" he asked.

If he was inquiring about her head, the answer was, "Better."

"Good."

He poured the eggs he'd beaten into the skillet, then he sprinkled grated cheddar cheese on top and covered the pan.

"Where did you get the bacon? I don't have bacon."

"It was hidden in the back of the freezer."

"Let's hope it's edible."

"I fried a piece and tasted it. It's fine."

"You're making an omelette in that big pan? I thought omelettes were made in little pans."

"You can do it this way, too."

"How do you know?"

He stopped for a moment and gave the question due consideration, looking as if he was hoping an answer would come to him and trigger a flood of memories. But all he did was shrug and turn back to the stove.

It was a small gesture, but it brought a clogged feeling to her throat. God, what was it like trying to puzzle your way through life when your whole personal history was a blank? Quickly pulling open drawers and cabinets, she set the table.

She felt his eyes on her before he grabbed the coffeepot and poured two mugs of the Jamaican blend that she liked.

Hannah added milk and sugar to hers. He took his black.

The domestic scene, his obvious vulnerability, her own response to him all made her suddenly uncomfortable. "Tell me again why you want *me* specifically to help you," she muttered.

"I investigated a number of candidates. You felt right."

He removed the top from the pan, and she saw that the eggs had fluffed and the cheese had melted. After loosening the omelette from the bottom of the pan, he cut it down the middle with the spatula, then carefully folded over each portion as he transferred it to their plates. After handing her one, he reached for the bottle of habanero sauce he'd set on the counter and liberally doused his portion.

"You like that stuff?"

"I found it in your cabinet. Don't you?"

"I keep it around for my Latin American friends."

He nodded, and she watched him dig into his breakfast. Apparently his tolerance for hot sauce was off the scale.

As she took a small bite of the omelette, her mouth was immediately flooded with flavor. "This is good."

When he smiled at the compliment, two dimples appeared on either side of his mouth. She looked away before she became too enchanted with the effect.

"You remember how to cook, and other skills, but you don't remember anything personal?"

"Sometimes I get a snatch of memory. I don't know if it's real or something I read in a book or saw on TV."

"Such as what?"

He set down his fork and leaned back in his chair. "The desert. The wind blowing against my face. A horse under me. Or it could be a smell. The smell of creosote bushes."

"What's that?"

"A plant that grows in the desert."

"Did you look that up in a book or did you just know it?"

"I just knew it."

"The desert must be part of your background."

"Probably. But I've stayed away from it. I figure if somebody's looking for me, that's where they'll start."

"I thought you wanted to be found?"

"Not till I know who's beating the bushes for a missing million bucks."

Last night he'd been evasive about his background. This morning she decided that he was trying to be as straight with her as he could, and that made a tremendous amount of difference.

"You don't remember any people?" she asked.

"I reckon not." She watched as he took his bottom lip between strong white teeth. "That's the worst part—the feeling of being totally alone."

If the statement and the gesture were a bid for her sympathy, it worked. But she couldn't afford to let him slip past her defenses. As one more test of his sincerity, she asked, "Are you willing to try hypnosis?"

"I don't know. What did you have in mind?"

"I've worked with a couple psychologists in the past. Maybe one of them can, uh, regress you to the moment when you lost your memory."

"I'm willing to try it."

"What if I find out that you're a criminal?"

"You can turn me over to the cops."

"Just like that?"

"You have my word I'll cooperate with the authorities, when and if we determine that's the right course of action."

"What's your word worth?" she asked.

His eyes turned fierce. "Everything. It's one of the few things I have left."

She stared into those dark eyes that seemed to dance with flames and believed him.

"Don't you want to talk about money? I mean your fee."

"Of course. I want a ten-thousand-dollar retainer," she answered, asking for an outrageous amount.

"You've got it."

"That's easy for you to say. It's not your money."

"Maybe we'll find out that it is." He shifted in his chair. "Don't keep me dangling. Have you made a decision?"

"I'll work with you—unless I come to the conclusion you're lying."

"I'm not!"

"Then we have a deal."

He pushed his empty plate away. "So now that's settled, let me ask *you* a question. Last night's attack on you—do you think it was random? Or does somebody have a grudge against you?"

Her head came up. "What makes you think so?"

"He shouted, 'Got ya, bitch,' like he meant *you.*"

She felt suddenly as if she were sitting in a cold draft. To cover the reaction, she said, "If you're appointing yourself my bodyguard, I don't need one."

"Don't you?"

She scowled because she didn't want to go any farther down that path. Changing the subject abruptly, she said, "Let me see if I can set up an appointment with Kathryn Kelley or Abby Franklin. They're both Ph.D. psychologists who work at 43 Light Street—the building where my office is located."

"You've used them before?"

"Yes. They're both excellent." Pushing her chair away from the table, she picked up the receiver from the wall phone and dialed the business line of Doctors Kelley and Franklin. Both had cut back on their patient load after marrying and starting families, which meant that they were often available for emergency sessions where other psychologists would be booked up.

As Hannah expected, she got their answering machine. So she left a succinct message.

It was Kathryn Kelley who called back while Hannah was washing the breakfast dishes.

"This is Hunter's day off at Randolph Security. So he's staying home with Ethan. I'm free most of the day, so pick a time."

Hannah tried to picture one of the tough-as-nails guys who

worked for Randolph taking care of an eighteen-month-old. But she had the feeling that Hunter was up to the job.

She glanced from the phone to Luke. "One o'clock?"

When he nodded, she confirmed the time, then gave Kathryn the name he was using.

"You know where the office is?" she asked after she'd hung up. When he nodded, she continued, "Then I'll meet you there at ten to one. And don't worry about protecting me this morning. I'll be fine."

"Okay. I'll see you there," he agreed, apparently unwilling to push the bodyguard scenario.

As soon as the door had closed behind him, she went back to the little room she used as an office and booted up her computer. The Light Street Detective Agency paid an enormous monthly fee for a very sophisticated database service that gave her information on a person's education, credit, arrest and medical records, among other things. But only if you had a confirmed identity—which she didn't have for Luke Pritchard. Still, she'd feel remiss if she didn't at least check.

As she expected, the search was a waste of time. There were thousands of individuals in the U.S. with that name. With a big concentration in Texas and Alabama.

Perhaps his fingerprints were on file with the FBI. Getting out her fingerprint kit, she slipped it into her purse, then changed into business clothes—comfortable slacks and a silk blouse—and started downtown. On the way, she stopped for a Reuben sandwich, which she ate as she checked her mail. But as one o'clock approached, she found her attention wandering. Stopping to consider the source of her disquiet, she realized that she was worried that Luke Pritchard might have changed his mind and wouldn't show up. And she would never see him again.

Damn, what had she been thinking? She'd been so eager to get the man out of her apartment that she'd shoved him out the door without even getting his local address.

She kept glancing at the clock, wondering if she should go down to Kathryn's early. But she kept herself from getting up until it was almost time for the appointment.

HANNAH WOULD HAVE BEEN even more disturbed if she'd known that Dallas Sedgwick was sending a squad of undercover operatives to Baltimore to look for the man she knew as Luke Pritchard.

But he wasn't the only powerful figure beating the bushes for a man and a suitcase full of money.

Addison Jennings was another contender in the million-dollar sweepstakes.

Like Sedgwick, he ran a powerful organization with scores of operatives at his disposal. But Jennings had a number of advantages over the crime boss. For one thing, from his secret headquarters in Berryville, Virginia, he was tapped into far more sophisticated sources of information, including the resources of the federal government. For another, he had a fuller picture of the problem and thus a name that he hoped would aid him in the search—Vincent Reese. Along with the name came a thick dossier.

Vincent Reese. Not the name the fugitive had been born with, of course. But he'd been using it off and on for most of his adult life, and the folder that Addison had accumulated bore that label.

Reese had first gotten in trouble as a juvenile and had been sent to reform school. The experience had hardened him, and he'd come out with a chip on his shoulder—and a well-developed sense of caution that had stood him in good stead since those formative years.

He'd managed to avoid arrest since that initial juvenile incarceration. But there was plenty of evidence of criminal activity. Or at least guilt by association. Reese might have done some fancy footwork to keep himself out of jail. But plenty of his buddies were behind bars. Those were the lucky ones. The less fortunate had ended up riddled with bullets— either at the hands of the police or in a gang war shoot-out. Which was apparently what had happened to the group found in the wasteland on the Mexican side of the Rio Grande last month.

Addison reached for his pipe, focusing on the soothing ritual of filling the bowl with tobacco and tamping it down.

Setting a match to the tobacco, he sucked in smoke, then let it out in a wreath around his head. The secret facility he headed might be a no-smoking zone, according to government regulations, but the prohibition did not extend to his office. Pipe tobacco was one of his few vices, and one he would continue to indulge.

The smoke helped to ease some of the tension from his neck and shoulders. A year ago, he'd stepped into the shoes of a man who was a legend in the intelligence community. A man who wasn't afraid to take on the tough assignments, because he saw them as his patriotic duty.

Amherst Gordon had died in the service of his country, pushing himself beyond the capacity of his frail body. He'd been a hero to the end. And he'd handpicked his successor to run the Peregrine Connection, the super-secret agency that took on jobs too sensitive for the U.S. government to openly acknowledge.

Addison had tried to decline the job, but his old friend had been unwilling to take no for an answer. And finally he'd shouldered the responsibility. Now he was doing his best to fill a pair of very large shoes, although sometimes he thought the job was more than one man should be forced to bear.

Like this present operation that had self-destructed in the desert. Lives had been lost—including one life he valued very highly—and he knew he bore some of the blame. Which was why he was looking for Vincent Reese. And why he was going to make the man explain exactly what had happened out there.

WHEN HANNAH WALKED into the psychologist's waiting room, she felt a tremendous sense of relief as she spotted Luke standing with his hands hooked into his front pockets and staring out at the Baltimore landscape.

She could see he'd showered and changed into fresh jeans and a blue button-down shirt—something a little more formal than the T-shirts she'd seen him in before, but not much.

He didn't turn, but from the way his back straightened she knew he sensed her presence. She was glad his back was to her so that he wouldn't see the look of relief on her face.

"Cities make me feel boxed in," he remarked, his drawl more pronounced than it had been the night before.

"If you're a country boy, why are you here?"

"The reasons I gave you before. Protective coloration."

The flat way he said it made a shiver travel down her spine. Before she could collect herself, the door opened and an attractive woman with wavy red hair and green eyes stepped out.

"I'm Kathryn Kelley," she said, holding out her hand.

Luke shook it. "I've been Luke Pritchard for three weeks," he allowed.

But the casual statement didn't fool Hannah. She could tell he was worried about this meeting and trying not to show it.

Hannah watched the Outlaw and the Psychologist sizing each other up. It would have been amusing if she hadn't been personally involved.

The silent observation brought her up short. Personally involved? In such a short time? And with a man she couldn't entirely trust?

When Kathryn stepped aside and gestured for Luke to come into her office, Hannah asked, "Can I come with you?"

"That's up to Mr. Pritchard."

"Luke will be fine," he corrected. "One of my goals is to prove to Hannah that I've got nothing to hide. So of course she's welcome to join us."

They all trooped into the office, and Kathryn indicated that he should sit in the comfortable easy chair with its back to the window. She sat opposite him, and Hannah to his right.

"Why are you here?" Kathryn asked him.

"Hannah thinks it's a good idea."

"You don't?"

"Just a gut feeling."

"You have amnesia?" the psychologist asked.

"Yes."

"Can you give me some background about the problem?"

Luke shifted in his seat and made an effort to relax his hands. Dutifully, he repeated much of what he'd told Hannah.

Kathryn remarked only when he finished. "My usual procedure would be to spend several sessions exploring your problems before getting into hypnosis."

"I don't have a whole heap of time," Luke pointed out.

"I understand your feeling of urgency," Kathryn answered mildly. "We can try hypnosis this afternoon."

"Good," he said, as though eager to get it over with.

"Then let me tell you a little about the technique we'll

employ. I use it regularly with people who have lived through disturbing events they can't recall. Really, it's self-hypnosis. And I'm just there to guide you back to an earlier time and help you control the experience." After giving him a fuller explanation, she asked, "Any questions?"

"No."

"Then make yourself comfortable."

He stretched out his long legs, crossing his booted feet at the ankles.

Kathryn pulled her chair closer. "Raise your eyes just a little and look up at the line where the wall meets the ceiling."

Luke did as he was asked.

"Now I'm just going to help you relax," Kathryn continued in a soothing voice. "If you could get away from your problems and go on vacation, where would you go?"

He shrugged. "I don't know. The beach, I guess."

"You like the beach?"

"I don't know."

"Well, it's a good choice. Imagine you're in a sling chair staring out at a beautiful blue ocean. The waves are rolling in, breaking on a horseshoe stretch of white sand."

Kathryn's voice was so soothing that Hannah could feel herself relax. Then she pulled herself up sharply and turned her head toward Luke. He was sitting in the chair, leaning back, his eyes closed.

"Can you talk to me?" Kathryn asked him.

"Um-hum," he answered in a slow, drowsy voice that accentuated his Southern drawl.

"How do you feel?"

"Good."

"That's fine. Do you want to try going back in time? Back to when you had a different name?"

He hesitated for a moment, and Hannah found herself waiting to see if he would agree.

"All right."

"Okay, imagine you're looking at a big TV screen across the room from you. It's got a calendar on it with this year. Can you see it?"

"Yes."

"We'll start by flipping the calendar back to this time last year. Can you see that?"

"No."

Kathryn frowned. "Okay, let's try going back farther, and instead of the calendar you'll see *yourself* on the TV. Let's go back to when you were ten years old. Can you see yourself on the television screen?"

"No."

"Let's go back a little farther. You're seven years old.

"Do you know your name?"

"Lucas."

"Lucas? Not Luke?"

"Lucas."

"What's your last name?"

"Daddy said I don't deserve his name."

Hannah sucked in a little breath. When Kathryn shot her a look, she pressed her lips together.

The psychologist was speaking to Luke again, apparently selecting a standard incident that most children would have experienced. "You've hurt yourself and your mother is comforting you."

Luke's head shook from side to side. Obviously agitated, he made a strangled sound.

"It's all right. Everything's all right," Kathryn soothed.

"No." His face contorted and his voice became higher,

more rural South. "Mama isn't here. She's gone away. When I asked about her, Daddy hit me." He raised his hand to his cheek, wincing in pain, and Hannah felt as if she'd been struck.

"Daddy says she's a little wetback slut, and she's not coming home again, so I should stop sniveling." His voice had changed so that he sounded like a hurt, bewildered little boy. The illusion was so strong that Hannah felt tears gathering in the corners of her eyes. His mama had left him, and he was in anguish. And his daddy was only making things worse.

"Everything's okay," Kathryn murmured again, in an obvious bid for damage control. Apparently this wasn't what she'd expected when she'd suggested going back into his childhood.

Moisture beaded on Luke's forehead, and he reached to swipe it away. His face took on the pallor of gray stone.

When he half rose from his seat, Kathryn leaned forward. "Just relax. I won't let anything bad happen to you. Let's go to another time. You're an adult now. Let's come forward to this month. April. Two days ago. Can you see yourself on the TV screen?"

"No." His voice was raw. When his dark eyes snapped open, they zeroed in on Kathryn.

CHAPTER FOUR

Hannah watched Luke push himself out of the chair. Making for the door, he yanked it open and strode into the outer office where he stood with his back to them, breathing hard.

Hannah sat frozen in her seat.

It was several minutes before Luke returned, his angry gaze pinning Kathryn.

"What the hell were you doing?"

"You remember the session?" she asked.

"Yeah. And I didn't like it much. I didn't come here for you to go pokin' in my childhood."

She spread her hands. "I couldn't get you to remember anything more recent. I thought that perhaps a childhood memory would unlock your past. Do you recall anything besides the incident?"

"The incident," he repeated, his voice not quite steady. "No, that's all. And that's going to *be* all."

Turning, he stalked out again, then out of the waiting room.

Kathryn gave Hannah an apologetic look. "I've never had results like this. I'm sorry. I tried to—"

Hannah cut her off. "It isn't your fault. It was my idea."

"Apparently his problem is more complicated than any of us realized. It sounds like he had a pretty traumatic childhood."

"Yes." Hannah stood. "I'd better go see where he went."

Hurrying after Luke, she caught up with him at the elevator. Her eyes focused on the slump of his shoulders, the tightness of his hands.

He was hurting.

How long had she known him? Less than twenty-four hours if you didn't count the time they'd spent eyeing each other across the Last Chance Bar. Yet her sense of connection with him might have spanned decades.

He had no past. And *her* recent past was a mangled mess. Perhaps that was what drew her to him, helped her understand what he was going through.

He didn't turn, and she was forced to step around him to see his face. As she took in the lost, wounded look in his eyes, words of apology sprang to her lips. "I'm sorry."

When he didn't respond, she felt another stab of remorse. Desperate to communicate with him at all cost, she took a step forward and clasped her arms around him.

He stood rigid for several seconds, then slowly let his head drift to her shoulder, his face turned away from her.

"I'm so sorry," she whispered again. "One incident from your past comes back to you—and it's something… ugly."

He gave a shuddering sigh. "You didn't know."

He was absolving her of blame, yet she couldn't suppress a small sound of distress as one of her hands rubbed small circles over the rigid muscles of his back and the other stroked his thick, dark hair.

He lifted his head and looked down at her. As she stared into the bleakness that filled his eyes, she longed to wipe away that look of despair, wanted it more than anything she had craved in a long, long time.

Some part of her waited tensely for him to pull away, to

deny the awareness that had been building between them since before they'd spoken—since those long evenings in the Last Chance Bar.

He stood unmoving, neither withdrawing nor giving his consent, making her feel as if she were poised on the edge of a dull blade. She had been dead inside for months. Now she felt more than she had any right to feel.

He could hurt her. She was giving him that power. If he pulled away from her, the wound would be butchery, not a clean thrust.

When she couldn't stand the uncertainty any longer, she raised her face toward his. There was a charged moment when she waited for him to back away. But he didn't move. Without giving herself time to consider the wisdom of her actions, she brushed her lips against his. It was only the barest contact, but she felt her body heat, felt the heat coming off of him as well.

Slowly she experimented with the sensations, rubbing her mouth back and forth against his, increasing the pressure, nibbling, taking his lip between her teeth, then easing up.

It was when she'd pulled back a little that she heard a sound well from deep in his throat, felt his mouth take command as his arms tightened around her.

The kiss went from tentative to flash point in the space of heartbeats. He angled his head, his mouth hungry and de-manding, so that she needed to anchor her hands against his shoulders and press her body to his to keep from swaying on her feet.

It was like being caught in a hot desert storm, she thought with the last shreds of coherence her brain possessed, the wind swirling around them so that the only hope of survival lay in clinging together. At the same time she knew that cleaving to him gave her only an illusion of safety. It wasn't the storm that had the power to sweep her away. It was the man.

Still, when he silently asked her to open her lips, she did his bidding, then shivered as his tongue swept into her mouth, taking possession as though she were a captive of war and he had every right to seize and plunder.

She gave him that right, her tongue sliding against his, tasting him with the same eagerness that he tasted her.

There was no space between his body and hers, yet she inched closer, overwhelmed by the feel of his chest and hips pressed to hers.

She forgot they were in a public hallway, forgot everything but the man who held her in his arms—until something hard and thin slapped her leg.

"Oh!" She jumped, feeling Luke's muscles go rigid even as her head snapped around to discover a young woman in the hallway staring in their direction.

Hannah felt her face heat at having been discovered in such an intimate position—until she realized that she was facing Jenny Brisco, the wife of one of her fellow cops. No, make that former colleagues, she corrected her muddled thoughts. Jenny, who worked at the Light Street Foundation, was blind, and the hard object that had slapped against Hannah's leg was the cane she used to guide herself around.

"Sorry, I didn't know you were there," she said.

"That's okay, Jenny. It's Hannah." She stole a look at Luke, who appeared to be as abashed as she felt. "We were just getting ready to press the elevator button. Uh, Jenny Brisco, this is one of my clients, Luke Pritchard."

"Pleased to meet you, ma'am," he drawled, his voice several tones huskier than usual.

Jenny was a fairly perceptive woman. When a smile flickered on her face, Hannah suspected that her friend had a pretty good idea what they'd been doing, even if she hadn't seen the action.

"We were on our way down to my office so I can take Luke's fingerprints," she said.

He tipped his head to one side, his eyes telling her that was the first he'd heard of her plans.

The elevator arrived, and they all got inside, riding to the next floor in awkward silence.

"See you," Hannah said to Jenny as the other passenger got out.

"Fingerprints?" he asked when the door had closed.

"It's the next logical step," she said, watching his reaction.

"Yeah." He stood facing her, unmoving, and she didn't like the look in his eyes.

"What?"

"If you want me to find another P.I., just say so."

She felt a giant fist grab her chest and squeeze. "What are you talking about?"

"You know damn well I shouldn't have kissed you like that. Or at all, for that matter."

The car stopped at her floor, and they stepped out. Unable to meet Luke's gaze, Hannah focused on a spot on the wall several feet to the side of him. "I think I'm the one who…initiated the contact."

Before he could answer, another one of her colleagues came out of a nearby office. This time it was Marissa Prentiss, from Adventures in Travel.

Usually Hannah loved the way she ran into her friends in the building. Today she was starting to wish she'd moved her office to an abandoned warehouse.

"Perhaps we could have this conversation somewhere

more private," Hannah muttered, relieved when Marissa only waved and turned the other way down the hall toward the stairs.

Hoping Luke was going to follow her, she headed toward the brand-new suite of offices occupied by the Light Street Detective Agency.

It was a far cry from the grubby squad room where she'd worked until a few months ago. The plushly carpeted waiting area was furnished with a couple of comfortable leather couches facing a desk where Bonnie Brennan usually sat. She'd come on board about the same time as Hannah herself, and the two of them had gotten to be friends. Today she was glad that the receptionist was temporarily out of the room.

Leading Luke into her private office, Hannah closed the door.

There was nothing personal about the space. Jo O'Malley, the agency's senior partner, had outfitted it with an oak L-shaped desk and bookcases, a bank of vertical files and four comfortable chairs—three in front of the desk and one behind it.

Hannah stood looking around, suddenly conscious that there were no pictures on the walls or the desk, no knick-knacks on the shelves, nothing that made the room anything but a generic work space. The only clue to her personality was what Luke had said about her apartment—she was a neatnik, with nothing out of place and folders stacked in squared-off piles on the credenza.

Luke said nothing as he looked around, but she was sure he was taking in the barren environment.

In order to put some space between them, she rounded the desk and dropped into the high-backed swivel chair. After several seconds' hesitation, he took one of the barrel-shaped visitors' chairs.

The red message light was blinking on her answering

machine. She tried to ignore it, since she didn't need a client listening in on whoever had left a message. But the red light flashing at the edge of her vision only added to her tension.

Then Luke asked a question, and the focus of her attention shifted abruptly. "This morning you ordered me out of your apartment. This afternoon you kissed me. Why? Were you feeling sorry for me?"

"Of course not! And I didn't order you out."

"It sounded like an order to me. But let's get back to what just happened in the hallway."

She made a frustrated gesture with her hand. She wanted to ask if the kiss had seemed as if it came from a woman feeling sorry for a man. Instead she answered, "It was an impulse. Maybe I was looking for a way to get closer to you. It won't happen—"

Before she could finish the sentence, a large male form filled the doorway of her office. Over Luke's shoulder, she found herself staring at her friend Cal Rollins. They'd gone to the police academy together, worked on the street together, made detective within months of each other. About the time she'd left the Baltimore P.D., he had, too. He'd taken a job with the Howard County Police Department and moved out there so he could be closer to his ailing father.

Now he had come to her office in the city in the middle of the day. That alone was significant, never mind the look on his face.

"Hannah, where have you been? I left you a message. When you didn't get back to me, I came to find out why."

"Cal, what's wrong?"

He shifted from one foot to the other. "Ron Wexler is dead."

"Ron is dead?" she repeated stupidly, aware that Luke's eyes had focused on her with laser intensity.

Cal moved several steps into the room. "He didn't show up for work this morning or answer the phone, so a couple of uniforms checked out his house. He was lying beside his car in the garage, with a bullet in the brain."

"No," she gasped.

Cal moved to her chair and hunkered down beside her. Luke was on the other side, with a glass of water in his hand.

She didn't know where it had come from, but she automatically wrapped her fingers around the cold glass and drank.

When she'd handed him back the glass, he asked, "Who was Ron Wexler and what happened to him?"

Before she could speak, Cal answered the question. "He was one of the other detectives assigned to the Turner investigation with Hannah."

"The drug case? Where the kid got shot?" he asked.

Hannah nodded, unable to dredge up any words.

Luke's voice was gritty as he continued. "Last night somebody came after you, and from the way it went down, I thought it was personal—not just a random attack on the street at night. Today another one of the detectives involved in the case is found dead."

"What?" Cal demanded, his gaze shooting from Luke to Hannah and back again. "Hannah was attacked?"

"Yeah. And I don't think it's a coincidence."

The two men stared at each other. "Mind telling me who you are and how you're connected with this?" Cal asked.

Hannah's gaze swung to her former colleague. "He's a client of mine."

"And who are *you?*" Luke demanded.

"Calvin Rollins, detective, Howard County Police Department."

"Well, thanks for giving Hannah the information."

The two men continued to glare at each other across her chair like dogs staking their territory.

"Cal," she said, struggling to keep her voice even. "I appreciate your coming to tell me. But I think I can take it from here."

"I came to warn you to watch your back."

"I will."

"I'm already taking care of that," Luke added.

"I thought she said you were a client," Cal answered, his tone pointed.

"I am. But I have the…right instincts to keep her safe."

Cal gave Luke a long appraising look.

"I appreciate your coming by," Hannah said again.

"Yeah. I'll keep you informed of any more developments."

"Thanks."

"No problem." Cal stood where he was for several more seconds, then turned and left.

When he'd closed the door to the outer office, Hannah breathed a little sigh. "You weren't exactly friendly to him. He came all the way down here to warn me."

"I appreciate that. But I was letting him know that I can take care of you."

She nodded, thinking in the back of her mind that it should have been Gary who'd come to give her the bad news. He was still with the Baltimore P.D. and would have gotten the same information—only sooner. Moreover, he was the one who had recommended her for the Turner task force. For a moment, her mind was far away, stuck in her recent past.

"You don't think what happened to you and what happened to Ron are connected?" Luke pressed.

"No. It was a coincidence," she said, because that was what she wanted to believe.

"Bull!"

She glared at him. "Are you telling me you've got some inside information?"

"No. It's just a logical deduction. Or a gut feeling. Either way, you're in danger until they catch the bastard. Rollins thinks so. That's why he came here to warn you."

She refused to believe it. "Whoever attacked me tried to strangle me. Then Ron was shot. That's hardly the same M.O."

"Yeah, well, he didn't succeed with the first method, did he? Maybe he came back to shoot you and saw I was in your apartment, so he went after one of the other cops. Waited for him to open his garage door and blasted him."

She clasped her hands tightly in her lap, trying to ignore his logic. But it made a kind of horrible sense.

"So you're not goin' home to your apartment. You're coming to my place."

Her eyes widened. "I certainly am not."

"I've hired you to do a job for me. And until you call it quits, I'm going to keep you safe."

"You're sure you can do that?"

"Yeah."

"Why?"

"Like I told your cop friend, I have the right instincts. Otherwise, the guys looking for their money would have caught up with me."

"A few minutes ago I got the feeling you were close to firing me," she said, and had the satisfaction of seeing him look uncomfortable.

"That was the wrong reaction."

She closed her eyes and leaned back in her chair. "Do you mind elaborating on that?"

"I reckon I was feeling sorry for myself, and I started speaking before my brain caught up with my mouth."

When she didn't comment, he went on. "I told you, I need you. I think you need me, too."

"If you're offering your services as a bodyguard, maybe I should be paying *you* a fee," she said in a dry voice.

"Nonsense."

"I'm not going to let you dictate how I live my life."

He sighed. "I'm not dictating. I'm trying to keep you alive. You're a sitting duck in your apartment. You'd be a fool to stay there and wait for the guy to come after you again."

She thought about that for a moment, silently acknowledging that he was right—at least until she had more information about Ron. But she wasn't willing to let the Outlaw make all the decisions for her. "If I go with you, we're stopping off to get some of my things."

"You can buy anything you need."

"I want my own stuff."

"Okay," he agreed grudgingly. "If you'll come along peacefully."

"Under duress, Sheriff Pritchard," she mocked.

"I'm not Sheriff Pritchard," he contradicted, but a little smile flickered at the corners of his lips, then disappeared before she was even sure she'd seen it.

When she pushed herself up, she was annoyed to find her legs were shaky. "We should go get my stuff," she said brusquely, trying to let him know that she was in complete control of her emotions.

"Didn't you come down here to get my fingerprints?" he asked, reminding her that she'd completely forgotten why they were in her office.

"Yeah, right."

The kit was in her purse. She started to pull it out, then changed her mind, raising her eyes to Luke's. She had an idea and wanted to test it out.

"How am I going to take your fingerprints?" she asked. "I mean, what's the procedure? Do you know?"

She watched him carefully as he considered the question.

"The latest technology uses a scanner, kind of like at a grocery store, to scan bar codes. But a P.I.'s office probably uses an ink pad or the chemical system where you roll the fingers over a moist pad containing a colorless, odorless, non-staining chemical, then roll the prints onto a card. Absolutely nothing shows up until the card is heated. Then the chemical reaction gives you beautiful clean prints. There are also pocket versions that don't require heat that work fairly well on the street."

She stared at him. "How do you suppose you know all that?"

He shrugged the way he had when she'd inquired about his cooking skills, but she could see an edge of excitement under his calm exterior.

"I think you're in law enforcement," she stated.

"I think a criminal is as likely as a cop to know what I just told you."

"Suit yourself." She pulled out the kit she'd put in her purse before she left home. "Sometimes when I want to intimidate a suspect, I use the messy ink method."

He laughed.

"Give me your right hand."

He complied, and she held his large hand in her much smaller one, vividly aware of his warm, slightly rough skin. She had kissed this man not long ago. And despite what she'd said, she couldn't turn off her reaction to him.

Awkwardly, she pressed his thumb against the chemical pad, rolling it from one side to the other, then pressing it onto the correct box on the fingerprint card.

He cleared his throat but said nothing, keeping his muscles relaxed, allowing her to do the work.

When she'd finished with the right hand, she went on to the left, repeating the whole procedure. By the time she'd finished, she was fighting a breathless feeling.

"I suggest you wash your hands before you eat," she said, hearing the thinness of her voice.

Silently he nodded and disappeared through the bathroom door. As she stood listening to the sound of running water, she concentrated on taking deep, even breaths.

Too much had happened in the past twenty-four hours. Too much was still happening. And she didn't know how to cope.

A few months ago she'd had the rug jerked out from under her, and she'd struggled back to some semblance of normality. Now Ron Wexler was dead, and someone had tried to kill her. And she'd be a fool not to be worried, even if she had given Luke an argument about it.

He appeared in the bathroom door, drying his hands on a paper towel. His posture was casual, but she was learning to read his face. Though he tried to keep it neutral, he couldn't hide the tension around his eyes and mouth.

"Are you worried about what the FBI fingerprint database is going to come up with?" she asked.

"The FBI doesn't work with P.I.s. Only the police. How are you going to get them to take a look at that card?"

"How do you know who they work with?"

"I just do." He gave her his maddening shrug again.

"That's another interesting fact, don't you think?"

"That and five dollars might be enough to get you a cup of cappuccino," he said.

She hesitated for a moment, then made a decision to trust him with some private information. "There are things we can do here at 43 Light Street that aren't strictly by the book. Randolph Security can get into the FBI fingerprint database."

"What's Randolph Security?"

"A company started as a spin-off of Randolph Electronics. Now it offers a wide range of security services including some they don't advertise. And the less I say about that, the better."

"I'll defer to your judgment, darlin'," Luke said mildly.

But she wasn't fooled for a moment. It suited him to defer to her judgment, so he was willing to do it. As soon as he didn't like the way things were going, he'd take control again.

She'd ponder that later, she decided as they took the elevator upstairs again to Randolph Security. The headquarters building was in Towson, but the company found it convenient to maintain a branch office at 43 Light Street as well as a secure research facility in western Maryland.

Jed Prentiss, Marissa's husband, was doing a shift at the Light Street office, probably because it gave him a chance to have lunch with his wife. While Hannah told him that she wanted the prints run as soon as possible, she watched him and Luke size each other up, the way Cal and Luke had evaluated each other a little while ago. This time she was in better shape to appreciate the mutual mistrust—and it struck her that in a lot of ways, Cal, Jed and Luke were very much alike.

They were all cautious, suspicious, take-charge kind of guys who were dangerous when provoked. But they all had a softer side as well. Cal had come running to warn her as soon as he'd gotten the news about her dead colleague. Jed was completely devoted to Marissa. And Luke had proved that protecting her was one of his top priorities.

When she caught the direction her mind was taking, she brought herself up short. Luke was protecting her because he'd also hired her to do a job for him and it was in his best interest to keep her safe.

"Whose prints are they?" Jed asked.

"Mine," Luke answered, hooking his thumbs in his pockets. As with Kathryn, his drawl became lazier as he drew out the syllable.

Jed's gaze shot to him again.

"And what's the purpose of checking them?"

Luke made an openhanded gesture. "Well, now, I'm in the unfortunate situation of not knowing my identity. I've hired Ms. Dawson to help me find out who I am. She's been bragging on y'all, tellin' me you can get into the FBI database."

Hannah struggled to keep her expression neutral as she took in the shift in Luke's mannerisms. If she didn't know better, she'd think he was a good ol' country boy just stopping in to pay a friendly visit on Randolph Security.

Jed swung his gaze to her, and she had the feeling he wished they were speaking in private.

"You want to ask me if I trust him," she said, answering the question in his eyes. "The answer is yes."

Jed nodded. Beside her, Luke relaxed a fraction.

"Then I'll be in touch when I get the results," Jed said.

They left the office and headed for the elevator again.

"Thanks for the vote of confidence, darlin'," Luke said as she pushed the button. "At least in public, since you're not feeling perfectly sure about our association."

"Neither are you," she retorted.

Hannah waited for him to continue the conversation when they stepped into the elevator, but he chose to remain silent.

"You can be pretty maddening," she said in a low voice. "And you haven't even paid me yet."

"Well, I can't exactly write you a check. I'll give you a wad of cash when we get to my place."

"Which is where?"

"I'd rather not talk about it here."

She might have pressed him, but she knew he had his reasons. "Are you parked in the garage?" she asked.

"Yeah."

She led him across the street to the four-story concrete structure. It was dark inside, darker than usual. Glancing up, she saw that the lights were out.

Luke noticed it too and stopped in the entryway.

When she started for her car, he put his hand on her arm. "Your vehicle is known. It's safer to take mine."

"Fine." She wondered what kind of wheels a guy with a million dollars at his disposal would buy. He'd selected a slightly battered four-wheel-drive Dodge Ram that he'd either stolen or bought from a downscale used-car lot.

As he leaned down to insert his key in the lock, a figure darted away from the other side of the vehicle and started running.

CHAPTER FIVE

Acting instinctively, Luke pushed Hannah behind the truck fender, then took off after the fleeing figure, running in a crouched position to make himself less of a moving target.

He saw the guy vault the wall at the end of the garage. As Luke reached the low concrete barrier, several gunshots plowed into a support post inches from his head.

The small pistol he'd tucked into an ankle holster was instantly in his hand. But the sound of running feet told him there wasn't going to be a shoot-out at the Light Street garage. In the next moment, a car engine roared to life and tires spun on concrete. Peering over the wall, he was in time to see a dark sedan careening around the corner.

A curse rose to his lips as he watched the vehicle disappear. It was too far away for him to get the license number, assuming it would do him any good.

When he looked to his right, he found Hannah standing next to him, staring down the alley at the spot where the car had disappeared.

"That guy was shooting at you!"

"Yeah." Hustling her back to the Dodge, he got down on his knees, carefully inspecting the vehicle's undercarriage. Then he tried the doors. They were still locked, which was good.

The bad news was that he heard the sound of police sirens in the distance.

His mind must have been functioning pretty well, because he remembered to unlock the vehicle and remove the garage-door opener. Then, keeping his voice low and easy, he turned back to Hannah. "This vehicle is known to the shooter, so I guess we're gonna take your car after all. Which one is it?"

Wordlessly, she pointed toward a blue Ford.

When she started toward the driver's door, he laid a hand on her shoulder. "I'll drive."

"Why?"

"Because I've already got a bunch of stuff to think about— like getting us out of here before the cops arrive. Giving you directions is too distracting."

Conceding the point, she handed him her keys. When his fingers touched hers, he felt the coldness of her flesh. He wanted to reach for her then, wrap her in his arms, but that was a luxury neither one of them could afford at the moment.

Instead he unlocked the car and they got in. There was a pocket in the door for maps where he put his gun to keep it handy as he started the engine and made tracks out of the garage, all his senses alert for trouble.

A man in a business suit peered around the entrance to the parking deck, glancing furtively in their direction. Luke tensed, but the guy only scurried toward a car several rows down.

Glancing in the rearview mirror, he saw a patrol car with flashing red and blue lights nose around the corner moments after he'd pulled into the street.

You're just a civilian going about his business, he told himself, fighting the impulse to speed up. *They don't know you came out of the garage.* Nevertheless, his hands gripped the wheel so tightly that his knuckles ached as he drove down the block at a sedate pace. He didn't let up the pressure until he'd put a couple of city blocks between himself and the garage, glancing frequently in the rearview mirror to make sure they weren't being followed. Finally, when they were several blocks away and he was sure nobody was tailing them, he turned to Hannah.

She was sitting with her head thrown back against the headrest, her face pale.

"You okay?" he asked.

"I should have drawn my weapon," she said in a flat voice. "That's the second time I haven't managed to do it on the street. Last night and today. Two for two."

"You pulled a gun on me."

"That was different. You—you were threatening me in my apartment. I had plenty of time to think about defending myself."

His vehement curse filled the car's small passenger compartment. "I'm not going to listen to you beat yourself up. Neither one of us was expecting this guy just now to start shooting. And you weren't in any position to fire."

"Does it bruise your male ego being associated with an ex-cop who wimps out in a firefight?"

"What the hell is that supposed to mean? Do you think I'm the kind of guy who looks for scapegoats when the hit man gets away?"

She shrugged. "Forget I said it."

He swung his head toward her again, taking in her pinched expression. "No. What's going on here? Are you talking about me or somebody else?"

"Drop it."

Luke might have reminded her that she'd started the conversation. But he knew when to cut his losses. Some male chauvinist had made her doubt herself. He wanted to know who, but as he'd pointed out earlier, he had other things on his mind at the moment. So he clamped his jaw shut and kept driving.

When he'd decided she wasn't going to say anything else, he heard her clear her throat. "I guess you were right," she said in a thin voice. "The guy who killed Ron *is* after me."

"I don't think so. The shooter was beside *my* truck. We didn't come here together. That makes it more likely that someone was after me, not you."

"Who was he?"

"It could be a random robbery attempt." He coughed to clear the sudden tightness in his chest. "Or maybe one of the *hombres* who wants his million bucks back has tracked me to Baltimore."

"You think that's likely?"

"I don't know. I've been careful. But we have to consider the possibility that somebody spotted me on the street."

She made a small sound that he took for agreement.

"But that doesn't cancel out my previous advice about not heading back to your apartment."

"If somebody's spotted you, then your place isn't any safer than mine."

"If they've made their move in a parking garage, I'm assuming that they don't know where I'm living," he argued, but he was thinking that she might be right. It was time to move.

After that, neither one of them seemed to have more to say, so he reached to turn on the radio, playing a little game with himself that he'd been playing since he'd woken up in Chicago. What tunes can Luke Pritchard name?

He found a country-western station and listened to a couple of oldies he recognized. Then he fiddled with the dial again and stopped when he heard a deejay speaking Spanish, talking about the song he'd just played. Then listened to a commercial for a Latin American grocery store.

"You understand that?" Hannah asked.

"Yeah."

"I'm only picking up some of the words."

"'We carry the products you're looking for,'" he translated. "'Masa harina, plantains, pigeon peas.'"

"What's masa harina?"

"Corn that's dried and ground. You mix it with water to make tamales and tortillas."

"If you say so." Hannah gave him a pointed look, then glanced away.

He'd gotten to know the city pretty well, so he took a circuitous route to the place he'd rented in Canton, then circled the block several times looking for anyone who might be watching the place. There were no signs of surveillance.

The furnished condominium was probably part of an urban-renewal project. There was a private garage underneath each unit. Using the remote control he'd rescued from the Dodge, he pressed the button that opened the door, then, mindful of the recent unpleasantness in Ron Wexler's garage, he paused to inspect the area. There was nowhere to hide in the small space, so he pulled in, then shut the door behind them.

"Wait here," he told Hannah as he got out of the truck.

She did as he asked, and he made a quick check of the town house. Until today it had seemed like a safe haven. Now he wasn't quite so confident.

When he found no evidence of an intruder, he motioned Hannah to follow him through the connecting door, across the rec room and up a flight of steps to the living area. As soon as she stepped from the stairwell, she started inspecting the plush furnishings. "You rented something like this on a short-term basis?"

"Yeah, from a company that specializes in renting to guys temporarily transferred away from home. I told them I was on a half-year assignment to a computer company in Baltimore, and paid for six months in advance."

She was still looking pale as she dropped to the sofa. So he got out the bottle of bourbon he'd bought and poured her a shot.

She stared at the glass and wrinkled her nose. "I don't like bourbon."

"It's good for what ails you."

Like a child forced to take a foul-tasting medicine, she tipped back her head and downed the amber liquid in a couple swallows. Then, thunking the glass down on the coffee table, she asked, "Are you going to show me the cash?"

"Yeah." Feeling his throat tighten, he turned away and headed for his bedroom, where he pulled a scuffed canvas suitcase from the top shelf of the closet. It wasn't the same suitcase that had initially held the money. He'd ditched that one in a Chicago Dumpster and gotten this one at Goodwill.

He felt the weight of Hannah's gaze as he came back down the stairs with the bag in hand. He wasn't sure why showing her the money made him feel so queasy. But it was like a guilty secret he'd been trying to hide, and this was the moment when he had to reveal it.

Keeping his face expressionless, he set the suitcase down on the coffee table, then pulled the zipper tab, half hoping that when he opened the lid, he'd find out he'd been mistaken all along.

But no such luck. The interior was crammed with neat stacks of bills, hundreds being the smallest denomination. Each stack was held together with a rubber band.

Hannah reached out and picked up a stack from the first row, riffling through the bills and whistling.

"What do you do with a fistful of thousand-dollar bills?" she asked.

"Take them to a bank, look innocent and ask for something smaller. Then get the hell out of town."

"Kind of inconvenient."

"I've managed okay."

"Very well, I'd say."

He pulled out a stack of hundreds, counted out fifty of them, then added five thousand-dollar bills and set it on the table for her.

"Got a brown paper bag where I can stash them?" she quipped.

He laughed. "No. But I can make a quick trip to the grocery store later."

"That's okay." She folded the cash and stuffed it into her purse, then asked, "Did this place come with Wi-Fi, by any chance?"

"Yeah. Nothing but the best when you're spending some other *hombre's* money."

"I'd like to borrow it to check out a theory that's rolling around in my mind."

The way she said it made his stomach tighten. "Don't you want to rest—what with your head injury and all the excitement today?"

"I feel fine and I want to work."

Figuring it was useless to argue, he took the suitcase upstairs again and brought down the laptop. After handing it to her, he started to sit down.

"Uh, uh, I work better alone," she said.

He wanted to tell her that if she was doing research on him

she could damn well let him watch. Instead he wheeled and went upstairs, where he lay on the bed with his hands behind his head. But he was too restless to simply lie there.

One of the reasons he'd hired her was her flair for mining gold in a pile of rubble. He ached to see what she was doing.

Instead, he sat up, unzipped a small suitcase and got out the dossier he'd assembled on Hannah Dawson. Besides the background information he'd dug up on her personal life, he knew a lot about her professionally, too. Probably she wouldn't like to know how much he'd found out about her. But he would never have hired her if he hadn't checked her out first.

He knew she'd gotten a degree in American Studies from the University of Maryland, then entered the police academy. Like all cops, she'd spent her rookie year in the patrol division where she'd drawn the attention of the detective supervisors. They'd used her initially for incidental undercover ops— street-level drug buys, prostitution-john stings, gambling busts, situations where a young, attractive, fresh face would be successful.

Then she'd graduated to long-term temporary assignments, where she'd continued to excel. The attention from the bosses hadn't made her real popular with the other rookies, but she'd made a few good friends in the department. Like Calvin Rollins, the guy who'd come running over to warn her about the Wexler murder.

Then an opening came up in the detective division, and she'd been put through the selection process, just like everyone else. But he got the feeling it was just a political paperwork drill. She'd been the obvious choice to fill the slot. So, she'd been twenty-six when she'd been promoted to detective.

She was pretty young, both in chronological years and by street-experience standards, but she'd been one of the stellar young troopers who are highly motivated, unusually intelligent and exceptionally dedicated.

That was what had attracted him to her in the first place.

Now his mind drifted beyond the facts—to deeper speculations about young dedicated cops like Hannah. He suspected that some jerk of a boss had pushed Hannah Dawson hard, or let her push herself too hard. That had set her up for a fall precipitated by the emotionally traumatic event of watching an eighteen-year-old bleed out on the street. Yeah, a scene like that would have a far greater impact on someone like her than your average patrol cop.

He looked toward the door. Hannah had told him not to bother her, but he suddenly couldn't cope with the notion that she was down in the living room doing the same thing he was doing up here—prying into his personal life.

Or trying to.

Too antsy to stay where he was, he put her file back into the suitcase then moved quietly down the steps, thinking that he might have a chance to read her expression before she spotted him. When he was far enough down the stairs, he ducked his head and looked into the living room. Hannah had kicked off her shoes and moved to the couch.

Apparently she'd been too tired to work after all, because her eyes were closed and her head rested on the pillow that she'd propped against one of the sofa arms. She looked so young, so vulnerable.

Her chest rose and fell in the rhythm of sleep, and he thought he should tiptoe back up the stairs and let her get some rest. Then he saw that she'd fallen asleep with the laptop on her rib cage. It was moving slowly up and down with the rise and fall of her chest as she breathed. But it had drifted to the right—ready to tumble onto the floor in the next few seconds.

He came down the rest of the steps in one fluid motion, rounded the coffee table and caught the two-thousand-dollar machine as it was about to fall onto the floor.

As his hand touched her chest, her eyes snapped open and focused on him.

"What?" she asked breathlessly.

"The computer," he said, lifting it out of the way and setting it on the table, his eyes never leaving her.

In that unguarded moment of first waking, she looked like a lost child. Last night, somebody had tried to strangle her. Today, one of her best friends had been gunned down in his own garage.

Luke had sworn he wasn't going to get personal again. It was too dangerous—for both of them. But the bruised look around her eyes drew her toward him. He leaned forward, feeling her breath warm and sweet against his face. Unable to resist, he brushed his lips against hers, ready to draw back.

But her hands came up and fixed on his shoulders, holding him where he was.

"Luke, I need to…feel like I haven't made a mess out of my life."

The bleak tone of her voice tore at him. "You haven't."

"But—"

He silenced her with the touch of his lips to hers again, this time increasing the pressure, increasing his own need for more.

Her mouth opened under his, and he was intoxicated by the taste of her, the texture, the sweetness.

Perhaps he needed the same thing that she did. Certainly he'd made some kind of mess of his life. He didn't know precisely what; he only knew that it didn't matter as long as he could hold her in his arms and kiss her.

Delicately, his tongue investigated the softness along the insides of her lips, stroking the sensitive tissue, making little sounds rise in her throat, sounds that sent the blood rushing hotly in his veins.

He angled his head, melded his mouth to hers and kissed her for a long time, his tongue prowling possessively over her teeth and upper lip, even as he told himself that was all he intended to do. But as the kisses became deeper, more intimate, a kind of desperation took hold of him.

He yearned for more. He had known that all along.

Lifting his mouth from hers, he kissed the line of her jaw, working his way downward to the slender column of her neck, the vee at the top of her shirt, kissing her there, then opening more buttons so he could press his face to the sides of her breasts, turning his head first one way and then the other to gather in as much of her sweetness as he could.

"That's so good," she gasped out.

So good. But not enough. Not nearly enough. He wanted to be inside her. Deep, deep inside. But first he wanted her as hot and needy as he felt.

Her bra was a wisp of stretchy fabric. He pushed it out of the way, then covered the small mounds of her breasts with his hands, molding her exquisite softness to his touch, the contrast with her pebble-hard nipples driving him close to insanity.

He sought those small peaks with his thumb and finger, watching her face, seeing how much she liked what he was doing.

"Don't stop," she moaned, her eyes closing as she arched into the caress, then pulled him onto the sofa with her. His body covered hers, their legs tangling on the cushions, his erection pressing against her leg. She squirmed under him, making the position more intimate.

Her breathing accelerated. Her hips rocked against him. And she spoke a man's name.

Only it wasn't his name. It was Gary. And the erotic spell was shattered.

CHAPTER SIX

Hannah knew the moment the word was out of her mouth that she had done something beyond terrible.

Gary. She had called him Gary. God, no!

Luke pushed himself up, vaulted to his feet and stood staring down at her, the shock in his eyes so palpable that she wanted to turn her face toward the soft cushions and hide.

Even in her dazed state, she didn't allow herself to take the coward's way out. Instead, she kept her gaze trained on the man standing in front of her looking so hurt and confused that she felt her heart turn over.

"Gary?" he said, his voice icy.

All at once she realized that she was lying there with her shirt unbuttoned and her bra around her neck. Turning her face away, she pulled her clothing back into place and refastened her buttons.

When she looked up again, he was seated on the coffee table, his knees practically touching hers.

"I'm sorry," she whispered, feeling as if she'd lost her center of gravity.

"Not good enough."

Her head jerked toward him. "What do you expect me to say?"

"I expect you to tell me why you were making love with me and called out another man's name."

She didn't want to talk about it, but she supposed she owed Luke that much honesty. "Because that's what we used to do," she whispered.

"You mean he's the only guy you can imagine making love to and I'm just a substitute?"

Unable to keep her eyes on him, she looked down at her hands. "No, that's not what I mean at all. I knew it was you kissing me, touching me. I wanted it to be you. Then I got lost…" She let the sentence trail off and started over again. "I used to come home from the precinct feeling burned-out and raw. And he'd make me forget about how awful it was dealing with murderers and drug dealers and burglars all day."

"Your Mr. Nice-Guy Gary would take you to bed so he could help you deal with the tension of being a cop?"

She felt her face grow hot. "That's a crude way to put it."

"How would you put it?"

"We cared about each other."

"You and Gary Flynn?"

Her eyes widened. "You know his name! What business do you have prying into my private life?"

"It would have been stupid of me not to do a background check on you before I hired you."

She folded her arms protectively across her chest. "Did your background check include digging into my sex life?"

"I didn't dig into your sex life. All I knew was that you worked with a senior detective named Gary Flynn. I didn't know he was bedding you, too, until you told me!"

She felt her insides go hollow, but she managed to keep her voice steady. "It was an adult relationship."

"Was he married?"

"How dare you! He was…separated. Well, he told me he was divorced. He did get divorced."

"You're twenty-eight and he's what—close to fifty? I'd say he was taking advantage of you, darlin'."

"I don't have to listen to any more of this."

"Fine." He stood and paced from one end of the room to the other.

She remained sitting with her jaw clenched, watching him wear a trail in the carpet. Finally he stopped and looked at his watch—then turned on the large-screen television set that dominated one wall of the living room.

"What are you going to do, find a wrestling match or something?"

"I'm going to watch the news."

The program hadn't started yet, but after five minutes, she was treated to a quick promo: "Shots were exchanged in a downtown Baltimore garage this afternoon. Police are looking for a man and woman seen leaving the vicinity in a blue Ford."

Suddenly cold all over, Hannah stared at the screen as a commercial for cat food came on. "They were talking about us."

"No kidding. The cops must have talked to that guy I saw coming in just as we were going out."

"We have to report what happened, tell the police someone was shooting at us. That we—that you—didn't fire any shots."

"I don't think so," he drawled, the tone lazy but the words edged.

"Why not?"

"When you're up to your neck in manure, you don't open your mouth."

She nodded tightly, taking his meaning. When the news came on, she leaned forward, listening for the lead story. It was the shoot-out at the garage across from 43 Light Street.

As a Baltimore police officer, she'd been involved in many cases that had made the news. But she'd always been on the other side of the fence, gauging the content for what it gave away. Now as she listened, she had another agenda—evaluating whether the report was going to lead the authorities to her and Luke.

The station had sent a camera crew and a reporter to the garage. First there was a voice-over as the camera panned the parking spaces. They saw Luke's car on the screen.

"Where did you get your license plates?" she asked in a strained voice.

"From a used-car lot."

Nodding, she turned her attention to the screen again—to a brief interview with the man who had seen them leave. He'd made the car, but his descriptions of the occupants left a lot to be desired. Hannah was a young woman with dark hair. Luke was tall and thin and also dark-haired.

They both sat through the five-thirty news, then the six o'clock, switching stations. But there was nothing more. At least nothing more that had been made public.

"I can phone Cal Rollins," she said. "He'll tell me if he's heard anything."

"Darlin', I think you don't want to give the police any clues to the identity of the woman in the garage."

"Then what are we going to do?"

He sighed. "I hired you to help me. Now I've got you in a heap of trouble. Until we unravel the Luke Pritchard puzzle, I think we'd better get out of town."

"Can I suggest a location?" she asked, anxious to keep him from going back to the previous discussion.

"Okay."

"Pritchard, Texas."

His eyes widened. "What? Where did you come up with that name?"

"A map of Texas on the computer. The population's a little over two thousand. I'm betting that's where you're from."

"Pritchard, Texas," he repeated, rolling his tongue around the word. "How, uh, did you think to focus there?"

"I'm a P.I. I was a police detective. I look for clues."

"Such as?"

"There's your accent. It's Southern. And the expressions you use. They're rural, homey."

"The South is a big place."

"Well, it's easy to narrow it to the Southwest. You speak Spanish. You can describe some cornmeal stuff I never heard of. You put hot sauce on your omelette. You told me you remember the desert and some plant called creosote bushes." She paused, knowing he wasn't going to like hearing about the last part. "And there's that snatch of your boyhood that we got when Kathryn hypnotized you."

His face turned ashen, but she continued in a low voice. "Your father called your mother a wetback. That's someone who crosses the Rio Grande from Mexico."

"So what?" he snapped. "I don't think my childhood is the place to start."

"It's the only place we have to start," she argued. "You *did* pick the name Pritchard. And there *is* a Pritchard, Texas, pretty close to the border, between Del Rio and Big Bend. You're drawing a blank on your recent past. If we go to Pritchard, maybe we'll meet someone who knows you."

"I'll think about it."

"What do you mean, you'll think about it? That's your best option."

"I'll think about it," he repeated. This time, instead of pacing the living room, he walked out the front door. Not a good idea if the police were looking for them, she thought.

But she didn't run after him to say so. Instead, she sat on the sofa, thinking.

She'd been numb for months, and she knew the numbness was a defense mechanism. Now she was feeling things again. Too bad the major emotions were pain and chagrin.

When he didn't come back after fifteen minutes, she got up and wandered into the kitchen.

Like the rest of the apartment, it was well furnished with quality accessories. And she could see from the half-full dishwasher that Luke had been cooking for himself. In the refrigerator were corn tortillas, sour cream and piquante sauce, and he'd stocked one cabinet with canned beans and chilies and other foods that supported her hypothesis about his background.

She hadn't done much cooking in the past few months, but maybe it would take her mind off the recent incident on the couch, she thought as she rummaged beside the stove and found a skillet. However, as she chopped onions and added ground beef, she couldn't stop herself from imagining how he must have felt when she said Gary's name.

She'd been writhing under him, for goodness' sake. She'd known it was Luke. She'd wanted it to be Luke. But somehow she'd flashed back to the way it had been with Gary. Because she'd been using Luke the way she'd used her previous lover. As a way to let off steam. She'd told herself she loved Gary. She'd realized after they broke up that it wasn't true.

Trying to cut off the painful thoughts, she stirred beans and piquante sauce into the pan and let them simmer. Then she layered the filling in a baking dish, alternating it with tortillas. The casserole had been in the oven for about twenty minutes when she heard the front door open.

Luke appeared in the kitchen doorway as she was drying

the skillet and wiping the counters, and she felt a flood of relief—mixed with an awful tightness in her chest.

"What are you doing?" he asked, standing with his hands in his pockets.

"Finding another way to work off some tension," she said, and was immediately sorry she'd put it in those terms. "I thought that if we had something in our stomachs, we'd both be in a better mood."

"It couldn't hurt," he allowed.

"It probably has to bake at least another ten minutes."

"Okay."

He went back to the living room and turned on the TV, but there was nothing new about the gun battle in the Light Street garage.

She set the table, then took out the casserole and set it on the stove.

"It's ready. I don't have a trivet, so you're going to have to serve yourself from here," she said, handing him a plastic-handled spoon and a plate.

He dished up a moderate helping. "Tamale pie?"

"I guess. I've had it at potlucks. I figured I could fake one," she said as she joined him at the table, watching him as he took a bite.

"You fake it pretty well." He took several more bites, and she was glad he was enjoying the food.

"Thanks." She forked up a small portion, chewing and swallowing carefully because the food felt like concrete as it hit her stomach. "You said we have to get out of town. I guess we can put off the decision about where we're going until tomorrow. Maybe since your first memories are of Chicago, we should go there," she offered, even though she didn't think that was their best option.

"Yeah," he answered, obviously relieved to be off the hook for the moment.

She took another bite of the tamale pie and managed to swallow it with less difficulty.

Some of the tension had been defused, but there was still too much unfinished business for her to feel comfortable. On both a personal and a professional level.

ADDISON JENNINGS looked up as his most trusted associate came into the room and took a seat opposite his wide desk. It was Constance McGuire, the woman who had worked closely for his predecessor, Amherst Gordon. Gordon had been the brains behind the Peregrine Connection, and Addison had inherited the mantle of director from his old friend. Now as he looked into Connie's eyes, he knew that there had been an important development in one of their far-flung operations.

"Good news or bad?" he asked, setting down his pipe in the ashtray on his desk. He knew Connie hated pipe tobacco, although she would never voice her objections.

"I wish I knew," she answered. "We've found a rowboat pulled into a stand of river cane along the Rio Grande about twenty miles south of Buenos Aires, Mexico. Vincent Reese's fingerprints are all over it."

"Which side of the border?"

"The Mexican side. One of our men went into Mexican territory without authorization from their government, as per your instructions."

"Any sign of Reese? Or the money? Or…" He let his voice trail off because he couldn't force himself to continue.

"I'm sorry."

Addison swore under his breath, then struggled to regain

his equanimity. "Okay, can you tell me how Dallas Sedgwick is doing in his search?"

"He's discontinued his Chicago operation and sent five more men to Baltimore."

Addison's eyes narrowed. "We have them under surveillance?"

"Yes."

"You think they know something we don't?"

"It's possible."

He reached out to rub the stem of the pipe. "I keep thinking there's some factor we don't know. Some wild card Sedgwick is holding. Let me know the moment it looks like his men are on to something."

"Of course." Connie made as if to get up, then changed her mind. Raising her head, she gave him a look that wavered between sympathy and sternness.

"Addison," she said gently, "we've lost agents before. That's part of the price we pay for taking on the dirty jobs that nobody else wants."

"*I* don't send people out on assignments on the assumption they're going to get themselves killed," he snapped.

Her gaze remained steady, calming. "Our agent knew what he was getting into," she said.

"How could he? I didn't realize the danger and I was the one who set this up. It looks like I'm the wrong man for this damn job."

"You're the right man," she said. "If you didn't care about your people, I'd be worried. And this still may come out all right."

He dropped his gaze, embarrassed by his outburst yet still wishing he could share her sense of confidence.

"I'LL DO THE DISHES," Luke said when Hannah got up and started to clear the table. "You cooked."

"Okay," she agreed, going immediately back to the computer. As he watched her pick up the laptop and move to the easy chair across from the couch, he was pretty sure she was thinking the same thing he was—that staying out of each other's way was a good idea. So when he finished cleaning the kitchen, he prepared to go back to his room for some heavy-duty thinking.

But she looked up when he stepped through the doorway to the living room, and he stopped.

"You don't want me going home," she said, "but I've got nothing to sleep in. No toothbrush, no toiletries. I need to make a trip to the store."

"No."

Her eyes flared.

"You're not going out by yourself, 'cause that attack in the garage could have been directed at you."

"Now you're arguing the other way."

"I'm playing it safe."

She sighed. "You want to chaperon me?"

"That won't work either, in case we're spotted as the couple leaving the garage after the shoot-out."

"I'm not going to use your toothbrush. And I'm not going to sleep in a pair of your jockey shorts—if that's what you wear." The minute she said it, he knew she was sorry she'd gotten that specific.

"Even if they're new out of the package?" he couldn't stop himself from asking.

She scowled at him.

"You can give me a shopping list."

"That's safer than my going out? What if somebody spots *you?*"

"I'll change my look."

"I can do that, too!"

"You don't have any other outfits, remember?"

Defeated, she heaved a sigh. "Okay." After giving him a list of toiletries, she asked, "I don't suppose you know much about buying women's clothing," she finally said.

He thought about it and realized he knew more than he was going to let on.

She stared off into the distance, not looking directly at him. "Underpants. Lycra or something similar. Bikini-style if they have them. Small," she finally said in a rush.

He kept his eyes fixed on his notepad as she continued.

"Some medium-size knit tops, something a little fancier than a T-shirt, if you know what I mean. And a pair of jeans, size six. I like the stretchy kind, if you can find them."

At least she didn't ask for an extra bra or tampons. He figured neither one of them could have handled those items.

He changed into a work shirt, shoved an Orioles cap on his head and beat a hasty retreat, glad to have escaped from the close quarters of the town house.

As he drove Hannah's car toward White Marsh Mall, he glanced frequently in the rearview mirror, but nobody appeared to be taking any notice of him.

His uneasiness resurfaced, however, as soon as he got out of the car and strode toward the discount store he'd chosen.

Annoyed by the attack of nerves, he sped up and down the drugstore aisles, throwing things into his cart. When he spotted a man in a navy blazer, striped tie and gray slacks watching him, he slowed down.

Security. Dressed like a gentleman. But still security, and Luke realized he was calling attention to himself, which was the last thing he wanted to do. With a silent curse, he slowed down.

Then he turned the corner into the candy aisle and pretended that his sweet tooth was the most absorbing thing on his mind.

He moved slowly up the aisle, then stopped short in front of the section with Reese's Peanut Butter Cups. Something about the candy drew him, and he pursed his lips. Did he like peanut butter and chocolate? He couldn't remember craving the combination, even though he did have other clear food memories. The tamale pie Hannah had fixed had been familiar and satisfying. So had the habanero sauce he'd doused over his omelette.

Chocolate and peanut butter didn't resonate in the same way. So why was he standing there staring at the candy?

"Reese's Peanut Butter Cups. Reese," he repeated softly.

Maybe it wasn't the candy itself, but the name. Unsure of his precise motivation, he reached for the orange package and stuck it in his cart anyway.

Then, since he and Hannah were getting out of town, he went to the luggage department and bought an extra suitcase.

The security guy stuck with him for a few more minutes. When he was confident he was no longer being observed, he headed to the ladies' department, where a saleswoman took pity on him and helped him select the knit tops and jeans he told her his wife was too busy to purchase.

But he could see a woman waiting for assistance, her foot tapping on the floor and her expression becoming more and more exasperated. So he relinquished the salesclerk and went off to confront the lingerie racks alone.

As soon as he saw the array of feminine undergarments, he knew he'd made a big mistake. He could feel his temperature rise as he imagined how each of them would look on Hannah.

Scowling, he reminded himself that she was only using

him as a substitute for Gary Flynn—then he ordered himself to concentrate on the mission. But there was no way to make the purchases quickly. There were too many choices. The fabric seemed to singe his fingers as he fumbled through the selection, looking for her size—and thinking about which ones would look best on her. Or more precisely, which ones he'd like to see on her. Because whether or not she wanted him, he still wanted her, he admitted with a silent curse.

By the time he was finished, he felt a thin sheen of perspiration coating his brow and an uncomfortable bulge in his jeans. Pretending vast interest in a rack of flower-decorated sweatshirts, he ordered himself to cool down. When he figured he wasn't going to make a spectacle of himself, he looked around to locate the checkout counter, then made a beeline for the front of the store. So intent was he on paying for his cartful of feminine clothing that he didn't realize he was in anybody else's way until a voice rang out inches from his head. "What the hell do you think you're doing, buddy?"

Luke found himself confronting a guy with narrowed eyes and furrowed eyebrows.

The man stood poised on the balls of his feet, his jaw jutting out, his arms bent at the elbows, and his breath coming quick and hard.

Beside him was a harried-looking woman pushing a loaded cart toward the register. Sitting in the jump seat behind the handlebar was a little boy, his face suffused with a kind of sick fear that was mixed with resignation. And Luke was swallowed up by the look in the boy's large, dark eyes.

CHAPTER SEVEN

For a moment out of time Luke seemed to change places with the boy who watched his father with such fear. Dad was going *loco* again. He was going to hit the other guy, like he did when he'd been drinking. Then people would be screaming and yelling, and Mommy would cry.

"Barry, don't!"

Barry. That was wrong. That wasn't his dad's name. It was...

His mind trembled on the brink of discovery. In that instant, he could almost reach out and grab the past. Almost.

But the moment slipped away like a small fish slithering out of a hole in a net.

"Barry, please."

The frightened tone of the woman's voice brought the date and the situation slamming back into him.

The man was answering her. No, he was mowing her down with his voice. "This lummox tried to cut you off. You were getting into that line, and he came speedin' in ahead of you like the Indy 500," the guy railed, his speech slurring slightly as his hands clenched and unclenched.

Luke bit back a curse. He'd been trying to keep his head down. And here he'd gone and antagonized some hothead jerk without even trying.

Holding up his hands, he struggled to look contrite. "I'm sorry, I wasn't watching where I was going."

"Yeah, right." Barry took a step closer, crowding him again, his chest puffed out like a rooster whose feathers had been ruffled.

Luke wondered if they were going to end up trading punches right here in front of the small crowd that was gathering.

"You come on outside and I'll show you what I do to jerks who think they can get away with crap like that," the man named Barry said.

Well, not in here.

"He said he was sorry," the woman breathed. "Please, Barry, don't start anything."

The man whirled, facing her, one of his large hands coming up toward his wife's cheek.

It was then that Luke moved, his own hand shooting out to catch the wrist, knowing by the yelp of pain that he'd come close to breaking the bone.

The man's eyes flared dangerously.

"Leave the woman alone," Luke growled. Over Barry's shoulder, he saw the security guy hurrying in their direction and cursed under his breath, wondering what he was going to do now.

He was carrying a concealed weapon. If the guard searched him and found it, he was in deep trouble. On the other hand, if he made a run for it, it was like admitting that he'd done something illegal—or was planning to.

Before his brain made a conscious decision, he turned and bolted for the door, abandoning the cartful of merchandise in the middle of the checkout line.

"Hey, stop."

He didn't know whether it was the guard or Barry calling him, and he didn't wait to find out. In seconds, he was out of the store and into the parking lot. Since stealth was of little use now, he pelted across the roadway, fumbling for the car keys as he ran, thankful that he had found a space near the door.

His heart still drumming inside his chest, he pulled out of the space and headed toward the mall exit. He was almost positive nobody was following, but he was thinking now that he needed to ditch Hannah's car. Because if anyone had seen him leave in it—or caught the license tag—an APB might go out to the police.

After getting back onto I-95, he took the first available exit. Within ten minutes he'd come to a strip mall with a slightly smaller version of the store he'd just fled. Once inside, he duplicated the purchases he'd made earlier, keeping his mind focused on the shopping instead of the other topics clamoring for examination. Like his reaction to the man—and the boy, he admitted with a grimace.

When he'd finally finished with the shopping expedition, he headed for a nearby neighborhood, cruising the streets to find a house that met several conditions—like a collection of newspapers on the front walk and an older car in the driveway. One he could hot-wire. He knew how to do that, he realized. Just one of his many chicken-rustler skills ready and waiting when he needed them.

He closed his eyes for a moment, clenching his mind against the thought. But it stayed lodged in his brain like a hot poker, although the pain wasn't exactly physical. It was mental torture—little bits of criminal knowledge that came back to him, confirming his worst suspicions about how he'd ended up with that suitcase full of cash.

Ruthlessly he cut off the unpleasant thoughts. Working on autopilot, he found a suitable car, hot-wired it and drove back to Hannah's vehicle, which he'd left a block away. Knowing she was going to be pissed at him for abandoning her nice new

Ford in some random Baltimore neighborhood, he threw the packages into the backseat of his stolen wheels before heading home.

It was a thirty-minute drive, and he deliberately turned his mind to the subject he'd been avoiding. His reaction to Hannah's suggestion that they go to Pritchard, Texas.

The name had seemed right when he'd picked it out of the phone book. But as soon as Hannah had added the word *Texas* after it, he'd felt his skin crawl.

She'd come up with that particular town by using the clues he'd given her, clues he hadn't even known he was scattering around. He didn't remember the damn town, but he knew with gut-wrenching certainty that he didn't want to go there.

And he knew why, even if he hadn't admitted it to her: he was afraid of what he was going to find out about his childhood. He'd come to her thinking that his main problem was determining what events in his recent past had left him with a hole in his memory as big as Montana and a suitcase full of money. He'd told himself he desperately wanted to recover his identity. But the idea of starting in Pritchard, Texas, made him feel like scorpions were crawling all over his body.

So just who the hell was he?

A man without a past. A man who didn't seem to *want* to know his past. Yet there were things he could deduce about himself. Like the way he'd known that Barry was getting ready to attack.

He'd read all the signs instinctively. And now that he'd seen them bloom on the guy, he could describe them accurately.

Not just the visual changes. He'd smelled the man's anger, although he couldn't describe the odor. But he'd recognized the very subtle yet distinctive scent.

He'd smelled that scent before. In a war? In a street fight? In an ambush? He didn't know, and the gaping hole in his knowledge made him pound his hands against the steering wheel in frustration.

CHAD CROSBY STOOD outside the paneled door of Dallas Sedgwick's comfortable den and ordered his heart to stop pounding. The screwup at the parking garage in Baltimore wasn't his fault. He'd given orders for anyone who spotted the man named Luke Pritchard to put a tracer on his vehicle—not gun him down.

But the guy in Baltimore had panicked when Pritchard had caught him beside the car, then chased him across the garage.

That wasn't Chad's fault. But he knew his boss might not see it that way.

Squeezing his hand into a fist, he knocked.

"Come in," Sedgwick called.

Chad carefully arranged his features before stepping into the den with a file folder tucked under his arm.

Sedgwick took a sip of his scotch and soda, then set the Waterford glass down on the end table.

"Yes?" he asked expectantly.

"I've got some more news from our team in Baltimore. We have an ID on the man from the bank video."

"Excellent."

"He's calling himself Luke Pritchard. Does that name mean anything to you?"

"No."

"Well, we've been studying the records of unusual real estate and rental transactions in the area," Chad continued. "It seems Pritchard has been posing as a computer executive on temporary assignment. He plunked down a wad of cash for a six-month lease on a town house in Canton. That's a neighborhood near the gentrified harbor area."

"You're sure it's the same man?"

"One of our operatives posed as a government agent doing a background investigation. When he interviewed the real estate agent, this is the description he got—dark hair and eyes, sharp cheekbones, narrow lips and nose, weathered skin. Six foot one. Southern accent. Self-confident." Crosby laughed, relaxing a little now that things were going so well. "The real estate guy thought he looked more like an underworld type than a computer executive. Still, he was willing to take his money."

"It could be him. Or it might not be," Dallas said.

Crosby gave him a little smile. "There is one piece of evidence that's pretty conclusive. Remember when you had his fingerprints matched against the FBI database?"

"We didn't find a match!"

"Right. But we have his prints in our own security files. And I've obtained some prints from the paperwork he filled out when he rented the town house. Paper is an excellent fingerprint medium. We have several samples, and they match. It's him."

The news seemed to send a jolt like an electric current through Dallas's system. "Good work," he breathed.

"Give the word, and I'll authorize a raid on the town house he rented."

"You've got it. And do it tonight. I'll be waiting here for a full report."

"Yes, sir." Crosby wheeled and marched out of the room, satisfied that he'd turned disaster into triumph. In a few hours, they'd have the guy.

AFTER LUKE LEFT, Hannah picked up the messages from her office machine. One of them was from Jed Prentiss. But when she called the number he'd left, he wasn't there, so she left a message saying she'd get back to him in the morning.

Next she tried to work at the computer, gathering information about Texas and checking airline schedules. But gradually her concentration began to fall apart.

Finally, aware that she had been staring unseeing at Luke's screen saver for twenty minutes, she set the laptop on the coffee table.

Doing some stretching exercises, she tried to work the kinks out of her neck and shoulders. But the tension remained. Glancing at her watch, she saw that it was almost ten.

God, Luke had been gone for hours. She'd expected him back a long time ago. Either that, or he should have called.

A dozen scenarios leaped to her mind. He'd been in a traffic accident. Gotten arrested. Or the guy from the parking garage had somehow caught up with him, and he was lying on the cold pavement in a pool of blood. A sound of protest welled in her throat, and she shook her head in denial. It wasn't Luke lying on the sidewalk. It was Sean Naylor.

Luke was all right. He had to be all right, she told herself, even as she felt tendrils of anxiety wrapping themselves around her windpipe, making it difficult to breathe.

When the phone rang, she jumped, then dashed across the room and snatched the receiver from the kitchen extension.

"Hannah, is something wrong?"

The man on the other end of the line was Jed Prentiss, not Luke.

Disappointment closed around her as if she'd just been blanketed by wet fog. "I'm fine," she managed to say.

"You sound stressed."

"I'm fine," she repeated, then asked, "How did you get this number?"

"Easily."

"But not legally, since I'm sure Luke has the caller ID function blocked." When he didn't deny it, she added, "I told you I'd get back to you. You shouldn't have phoned me here."

Ignoring the comment, he asked, "Are you alone?"

"Do you mean, am I with Luke?"

"Yeah."

"He's out."

"Okay. I checked the FBI IAFIS fingerprint database. The prints you gave me aren't on it."

"Which means he's not a criminal!"

"Maybe. But there are over three hundred million people in the U.S. and the database only has a fraction of them," Jed retorted. "In addition, it's only ninety-two percent accurate. Maybe he's never been caught red-handed. Or maybe he's got a record in a state that hasn't transferred their files to the feds."

Although she couldn't see Jed's face, she could hear the disapproval in his voice. "That's not a very charitable interpretation."

"You didn't come to me for charity, did you?"

"No."

"Hannah, I don't like what you're doing."

"What aspect exactly? Taking Luke on as a client?"

"You're putting your life in this guy's hands."

"I told you, I trust him."

"Do you want to tell me about the item on the evening news, the one about the young woman with dark hair and the tall, thin guy who were seen driving away from the Light Street garage after gunshots were exchanged? The incident took place ten minutes after you left Randolph Security."

She made an effort to keep her voice even. "He's not tall and thin."

"Tall. You know, I kind of thought I heard shots. Then I convinced myself it must be something else. But there was an exchange of fire at the garage next door, and you were in it, weren't you, Hannah?"

"It wasn't an exchange of fire. Some guy shot at Luke then got away."

"And you still want to hang out with him?"

"Yes."

"Hannah, I know your location. I can come over there and get you."

While he was speaking, she heard the garage door open and said hurriedly, "Please, Jed, don't interfere. Thank you for checking the fingerprints, but if I need any more help from you or Randolph Security, I'll ask for it."

"Hannah, let's talk about this."

"No. I want your word that you won't do anything on your own. You and anybody else at Randolph." She thought for a moment. "And don't phone Cal Rollins either. Or anybody at the Baltimore P.D."

"Hannah!"

"Your word."

"All right," Jed answered grudgingly.

"Say it."

"You have my word I won't interfere."

She was still holding the phone when Luke walked into the room carrying an armload of packages. As he set them down, his eyes zeroed in on the receiver in her hand.

She reached out and set it back into the cradle.

"Who were you talking to?" His voice was edgy.

"Jed."

"Why did you call him from here?"

She forced herself to keep her hands at her sides, when she

wanted to fold them defensively across her chest. She hadn't done anything wrong, and she wasn't going to act guilty. "I didn't call him. I picked up a voice-mail message from him and tried to call him back," she said, enunciating carefully. "When he wasn't there, I said I'd talk to him in the morning."

"Did you leave your number?"

"No."

"But he got back to you anyway."

She swallowed. "Yes. He phoned me. But I made him promise he wouldn't interfere with us. And I trust him," she added.

"I don't."

"Apparently the feeling's mutual."

"Well, that's just perfect, isn't it? What did he want? Was he trying to make sure I hadn't murdered you in your sleep?"

"He was calling to tell me what he found from the FBI database."

Luke was instantly alert. "And?"

"You're not in it."

He let out the breath he must have been holding. "That's something, anyway. But not much."

"It means you haven't been arrested. At least as an adult."

"Right. Unless somebody's pulled my prints from the files."

"Who would do that? Who *could* do it?"

He shrugged. "If I knew that, maybe I'd remember who I am."

She stared at him, thinking that he'd taken control of the conversation before she'd gotten a chance to register her own concerns. "Instead of focusing on Jed, why don't we talk about where the hell you've been for the past few hours? Didn't it enter your brain that I might be worried about you? Don't you have a cell phone?"

He sighed. "No. And I kind of had my hands full."

"How difficult can it be to pick up a few items?"

"Not all that difficult. Unfortunately I attracted the attention of the store's security."

She caught her breath. "What happened?"

"You want the long version or the short version?"

"The whole thing."

He started to cross to one of the chairs. Then a noise outside made him go rigid. "What was that?"

"I didn't hear anything."

He stood very still, listening.

"You were going to tell me what happened at the store," she prompted.

"In a minute." Reaching for the remote control on the end table, he switched on the TV.

She was about to say it was way past time for the news when he pressed a button and the scene switched from the commercial channel to four different pictures—all views of the town house and its environs. One showed the garage. Another the street. Two more focused on the small front and back yards.

What Hannah saw made her heart leap into her throat and block her windpipe. Men dressed in black, their faces shaded by baseball caps, were on the front lawn, approaching the garage door. The back and front yards were clear.

Luke reacted instantly. "Come on."

She went stiff for an instant.

"Get moving!" he growled.

The sharp tug on her arm and the tone of voice unfroze her.

Holding tight to her hand, he raced for the stairs, and she stumbled after him. When she tripped and sprawled across the risers, he hoisted her up and kept moving.

They reached the second floor, which she hadn't seen until now, and sped down a short hall to what must be his bedroom. Flinging open the closet, he grabbed the suitcase with the money and a smaller bag before shoving open a bedroom window. In front, the house was three stories tall to accommodate the garage. But it was built into a hill. In back they were only two floors above the ground, with the kitchen bay window directly below them, she saw as she looked down apprehensively. Probably that was why he'd selected this bedroom, she thought.

"You first," he said.

"I—"

"I'm not climbing out and leaving you."

She might have thought he was looking out for her welfare, but the tone of his voice suggested a different motive. He didn't trust her to come along.

"Luke…I—"

A loud noise like a door being kicked in from below made them both stiffen.

"Get going," Luke snapped.

She put one foot outside, then the other, stretching down as far as she could to reach. Her feet still didn't touch the window projection, so she had to let go, falling several feet and barely catching herself against the rear wall.

Something flew past her and landed with a thunk on the ground. The suitcase with the money. The other bag had barely hit the ground before Luke was lowering himself to the bay-window roof beside her.

Inside, she could hear sounds of men's voices now. Angry voices. Ignoring them, Luke helped her to the ground.

Automatically, she picked up the smaller suitcase. He took the one with the money and they sprinted through the back gate and down the alley.

Above the sound of her pulse pounding in her temple, she tried to listen for the sound of footsteps pounding after them. Or gunshots.

But they seemed to have gotten away clean. When they reached the end of the block, Luke stopped her forward progress, waiting in the shadows until he was sure the coast was clear. Then they crossed the street and dashed into the next alley. They traveled in that fashion for several blocks until her lungs were burning and a sharp pain stabbed into her side. Then, as they came around a corner, Luke spotted a man get out of his car in front of a house, leaving the engine running.

"Some luck for a change," Luke commented, and she knew what he was going to do.

When the guy disappeared inside, he grabbed her hand again. "Come on." Without giving her time to protest, he leaped toward the vehicle, opened the passenger door and shoved her inside. Then he slid behind the wheel and sped off into the night.

Leaning back against the seat, she struggled to catch her breath. Maybe Luke wasn't in the FBI database now, but he would be if the police caught up with them tonight.

AWARE THAT he was hunched forward, Luke sat up straighter and tried to ignore the acid pain in his gut.

If he hadn't been constantly psyched for trouble, things would have turned out a bit differently.

"So it looks like the guys who are chasing the money found you," Hannah said.

"You think so? I reckon that was your friends from Randolph Security."

Her head whipped toward him. "That's crazy! Jed wouldn't do anything like that."

"This ain't my first rodeo, darlin'. What was his plan? To scoop me up and turn me over to the police, or interrogate me himself?"

"Jed wouldn't do either of those things!"

Luke flicked her a doubtful look, seeing the tautness in her face and shoulders.

"Even if they knew about the money, Jed wouldn't come after me like that. He doesn't need a million dollars."

Her voice rang with certainty, but in the moment he'd seen the men outside, he had stopped trusting her or anyone else. He drove for several more miles, then, figuring it was safe to stop, pulled to the curb and cut the engine, studying her in the light from a street lamp.

She raised her chin. There were two ways for her to go—weepy or belligerent. Apparently she'd chosen the latter. "If you're still thinking I had something to do with what happened back there, you're…you're nuts."

"What am I supposed to figure? I come home, you're on the phone, and you hang up. The next thing I know, an assault team pulls up. Would you take that for a coincidence?"

"I didn't call them in. I wouldn't do that."

"What would you think if you were me?" he demanded.

"Maybe I'd be suspicious," she conceded.

"Yeah." He didn't know what else to say. He wasn't about to admit it was possible he'd gotten a bit paranoid. In fact, he really didn't know what the hell to think. All he knew was that his nerves were strung tighter than a rope clothesline after a soaking rain.

It appeared that the woman next to him didn't know when to cut her losses. "If I'm in on it, why would I stick with you?" she asked.

"I didn't give you an option."

She made a disgusted noise. "I could have given you the slip if I'd wanted to, but okay, have it your way."

The tone of her voice might have convinced him. But he was in no mood to be convinced. He'd made himself vulnerable to her, been too eager to give her his trust. Now he was overcompensating, erring on the side of caution. The way he saw it, he had no other choice.

CHAPTER EIGHT

As he'd done before, Luke headed for a residential neighborhood. Feeling as if he was in one of those movies where the main character is doomed to repeat the episodes of his life, he started looking for a house where the occupants were away and also owned an old car. Forty minutes later, they had changed vehicles to something safer—a fifteen-year-old Mustang.

"Where did you learn to hot-wire a car?" Hannah asked in a conversational tone.

"Maybe I was a juvenile delinquent."

"Maybe."

He drove on into the night, silent until she asked another question. "Where are we going?"

"Gunpowder State Park."

"Why?"

"Maybe I'm planning to kill you and dispose of the body."

She gave a nervous laugh.

Letting her stew, he stopped at one of those huge supermarkets where you could buy everything from hot dogs to hardware—at any time of the day or night. When he came out again, he had a change of clothing for her, an extra toothbrush and bandages for the bump on her head, as well as a box of heavy-duty plastic bags and a shovel. The other things he needed were in the case he'd kept packed for emergencies.

It was lucky he was a millionaire, he thought. This was his third trip to a store that evening.

Next to him, Hannah was silent, and he was glad she was smart enough to keep her mouth shut. He didn't want to talk to her. He just wanted to get rid of the money and get the hell out of Baltimore.

Almost as soon as he'd arrived, he'd started making contingency plans for the cash because he'd known it might be dangerous—or foolish—to keep it with him.

He'd given himself several options. Tonight, Gunpowder State Park was the closest location.

Making sure to stay within the speed limit, he drove to one of the park entrances, pulled off the road and inspected the area. At this time of night, the park entrance was blocked by a chain. But removing it so that he could drive through was no problem. Once he'd replaced the barrier, he drove slowly with his lights off to the spot he'd picked out.

Hannah was sitting with her arms folded across her chest. "You're going to be able to find this place again?"

"There are dead solid landmarks," he informed her, but didn't bother to elaborate. One was a sign announcing the speed limit. Twenty yards farther on was a parking lot with picnic tables, and three big rocks between the grassy area and the woods. He pulled into a parking space, opened the back door and took enough cash out of the suitcase to meet their short-term needs. Then he closed the case again and wrapped it in several of the plastic bags.

"It's in your best interest to let me know if anyone comes along," he said.

She glared at him, but gave a tight nod.

Picking up the suitcase and the shovel he'd bought, he headed around the rocks and into the woods to a place where a log had fallen across the forest floor.

The physical labor of digging in the soft dirt helped work off some of his tension. It felt good to scoop up the earth and pile it in a neat mound. He made the hole deeper than he needed for the suitcase.

A grave, he thought. For the money. And if he got killed, nobody would ever find it.

Cutting short the morbid thoughts, he set the suitcase inside and re-covered the pit, hiding the evidence of his handiwork by spreading the extra dirt around the area and covering the raw earth with leaves and other debris. After checking the results with a flashlight, he wiped his hands on his jeans and returned to the car.

AS THEY PULLED AWAY from the parking area, Hannah kept her eyes straight ahead, unwilling to ask Luke exactly where he'd hidden the cash.

They drove for several miles before she couldn't stand the uneasy silence any longer. "So now that the money's taken care of, what next?"

He sighed. "We're heading for Pritchard, Texas."

"I thought you didn't want to go there."

"I've changed my mind."

"Why?"

"You were right. It's the only place I have to start."

"Did you come to that conclusion before or after the men outside?"

"Before."

She stole a glance at him, wondering what had happened to change his mind. But if he wasn't going to volunteer the information, she wasn't going to pry.

"So we're going to the airport?" she asked instead.

"Yeah. The Philadelphia airport. Where we catch a plane for San Antonio."

"That's two hours from here."

"But a lot safer than Baltimore/Washington International, if the cops—or the guys who showed up at the town house—have staked out the local airports."

Although his caution was prudent, she was quick to point out a flaw in the plan. "A picture ID is required to get on a plane. So they'll have Hannah Dawson made when we show up at the ticket counter."

He turned to her for a second, then back to the road. "I've got a second identity for me and a fake ID for you. In the name of Helen Davis, so it won't be too hard to remember."

Her head whipped toward him. "What? When have you had time for anything like that?"

"I ordered it before I approached you with the job offer."

She took several seconds to digest that startling piece of news. "That could have been a big waste of money."

He merged into the traffic on Harford. "I've got *dinero* to burn, remember?"

She nodded absently, her mind on the implications of his previous statement. He'd ordered the ID before he'd asked her to work for him, which meant he'd been sure of her, and sure of his own decision to hire her. That was no longer true. His faith in her had been eroded, and she found the knowledge had left an aching hole in her chest.

"If you don't trust me anymore, why are you taking me with you?" she asked.

"You know my plans. If you've already talked to your friend, you could do it again."

"I didn't! I mean we only talked about the FBI database.

And I told Jed that I trusted you when he tried to tell me I was making a mistake by sticking with you. That was all."

His shrug had her blood boiling. They rode in strained silence until she heard Luke mutter something she was glad she couldn't quite catch. Sitting up straighter, she looked from him to the road. "What?"

"Up there!"

He pointed toward the road ahead, where she could see several police cars with flashing lights. Ahead of them the line of traffic was slowing down.

"An accident?" she asked.

"Or a roadblock." Luke looked behind him.

"What are you doing?"

"Figuring out how to turn around."

"You can't. They'll come after you."

Probably he'd known she was right all along. Still, he made a frustrated noise. When the car in back of him honked, he inched forward. At the same time, his hand slid down and came out with the gun he'd tucked under his shirt.

Her skin turned icy. "Luke, put that away. If they see that, then you will be in trouble."

"What am I supposed to do," he growled, "just let them scoop me up?"

Always before he'd been calm, in control. But it was obvious that the day's events had been too much for him.

She strained her eyes, trying to see what was going on up ahead. But it was too dark to tell. Still, she kept her voice calm and even as she said, "Luke, it could just be an accident and people are slowing down to look. Or maybe they're spot-checking for drunk drivers."

He craned his neck and clenched his teeth when he

couldn't see what was happening. She was in the same position as she sat with her nails digging into the seat cover.

"What if they're looking for us, for me?" he demanded.

"Why would they be looking for us?"

"This car is stolen, remember."

She felt the air freeze in her lungs. Somehow she'd forgotten about that little detail.

Rising up in her seat, she strained to see what was going on. Then she spotted cars on either side of the road. Cars with crumpled hoods and rear ends. Then an ambulance came into view.

"It's an accident," she breathed. "Just an accident."

Moments later, they reached the site and rolled slowly past. Then they were speeding up again, leaving the bottleneck behind them.

"That took a couple years off my life," she commented.

"Yeah. I've had enough excitement for one day."

She agreed as she leaned back in her seat and closed her eyes. With an effort, she tried to turn her mind to constructive channels—tried to see the raid on the town house from Luke's point of view. He didn't know who he was, he'd picked a detective to help him find his identity, and he'd trusted her enough to talk about his dangerous situation.

Then at the worst possible time, she'd called him by another man's name. Next, the house he'd thought was safe had been attacked—after she'd made a phone call he was sure had compromised his security.

He hadn't listened when she'd denied working with Jed. But what if she opened up a subject that he knew was painful for her—would that make a difference in his attitude?

Her mouth turned dry, but she managed to say, "Do you know what it's like for a detective on the fast track?"

"No. But I assume you're about to tell me."

She moistened her lips. "It's exciting at first. Then it's grueling. It burns you out. I saw hot-shot guys who turned into discipline problems or who got into alcohol or drugs or dug themselves into deep financial problems. I knew I was headed for some kind of crash—until Gary and I…"

She let the sentence trail off, then started again. "He was my mentor. He helped train me. I told him my problems, went to him for advice, and it was tremendously flattering when he showed a personal interest in me. After a while, I needed the stability he gave me. It was the one constant in my life."

"You let him get close to you. And he used the opportunity to get you into his bed. So where is he now? What happened when you really needed him after the shooting?"

Luke had cut to the bone with the precision of a surgeon. Maybe because she hadn't talked about this with anyone, she found herself answering the question. "At first he comforted me. Then after a couple of days when I was still too shaky to go to work, he ordered me to snap out of it." She swallowed, forced herself to tell him the worst part. "He said, 'Suck it up and get over it, Troop. If you don't want to shoot bad guys, quit and go to work at Burger King. Then you can have it your way. Until then, stop whining and get your ass back out on the street where it belongs.'"

Amazed that she'd repeated the words she had never uttered to anyone else, she sat in frozen silence in the moving car.

His curse made her flinch. "The polecat had the nerve to say that to you?" Detaching his right hand from the wheel, he circled her forearm with his fingers, then worked his way down to the back of her hand.

She closed her eyes, absorbing the feel of his flesh pressed to hers. The contact didn't make it any easier to say the next part. "I felt like I'd failed him."

Again Luke's angry rejoinder rang in the confined space. Then more quietly he said, "It wasn't your fault. He should be horsewhipped for using you. And horsewhipped for leaving you when you needed him most."

"I was the one who drew him into the relationship in the first place. Don't you understand? I liked the prestige of being his girlfriend. Then I needed his strength."

"You sound like a rape victim blaming herself for getting attacked."

"It's not the same. He didn't force me into anything. I flirted with him. I invited him to dinner at my apartment and had a sexy nightgown tucked in the bureau drawer…"

"And you ended up in the bedroom. That night and a lot of nights after that."

She kept her moist palm pressed to her thigh. With brutal honesty she said, "I was doing it again with you. That's the way I act with men. Needy and seductive. I'm sorry."

"How many other men are you talking about?"

She looked down at her lap.

"He was the first one, wasn't he?"

"How do you know?" she whispered.

"You're a lot more innocent than you think. You don't know how you are with men because you've only been with one. The one who seduced you because *he* liked the sex and he liked having you for a trophy. *He* liked everybody knowing that he was sleeping with Miss Detective on the Fast Track. I'll bet he didn't keep it a secret around the station house, did he?"

She had never thought about it in those terms. But she

didn't have time to turn it over in her mind, because Luke was speaking again.

"And then there's the other guy. The one who can't remember who he is."

Startled, she turned to stare at him, but his rigid profile gave nothing away. Before her brain had time to catch up with her mouth, she said, "So why exactly did *you* get close to me? Because you want to forget the mess you're in?"

"That's as good a reason as any," he bit out, and she realized a few seconds too late that the question had been a mistake.

Beside her, Luke lapsed into silence, and Hannah wished she hadn't started the conversation in the first place. It certainly hadn't helped.

Shifting in her seat, she watched the lights passing and tried to will the tension out of her body. She told herself she'd succeeded—until they pulled into a motel parking lot about twenty minutes from the Philadelphia airport.

Not wanting to make the decision about sleeping arrangements, she was willing to let Luke go in and register. But he insisted on ushering her into the lobby with him while he got a room on the third floor—with two queen-size beds.

One room. Where he could keep an eye on her, she thought as she watched him slip the chain into place.

She was pretty sure she could get away from him if she tried. But that wasn't what she wanted.

What did she want? she asked herself as she washed her face and brushed her teeth. For the immediate future, she wanted to stay with him. To prove that he was dead wrong about his new assessment of her.

And then what?

That part was complicated. Dangerous. It made her feel as

if she was standing at the edge of a crumbling cliff. So she backed up to more solid ground and pretended to herself that she hadn't come to any decisions.

But the way he was keeping his distance from her hurt. Even when she washed her hair and asked him to replace the butterfly bandage on her head, his touch was so mechanical that she wondered if she'd only been imagining any sort of intimacy between them.

"Are you going to handcuff me to the bed?" she asked when she saw him standing hesitantly, looking toward the shower, looking as though he was wondering whether it was safe to close the door.

"That would be a good idea. But I don't have any cuffs." He made a snorting sound. Then slammed the door and took the quickest shower on record.

She had turned off all but one of the lamps and was lying in one of the beds when he came out wearing only his jeans, his chest bare and hair still glistening with droplets of water.

His gaze zeroed in on her, pinned her for a brief moment, and she wondered if he really thought she was going to jump ship. Or whether he had simply switched into some sort of protective mode where he wasn't prepared to rely on anyone but himself.

She understood that. Understood what he must be feeling. And she longed to convince him that she really was on his side. But she didn't see any way to accomplish that goal—besides showing him she was prepared to cooperate with any plans he had.

Unless she judged them outrageous or just plain foolish, she silently added.

She watched him as he called the airline and booked a flight for the next morning. Then after hanging up, he curtly informed her that they were getting up at 4:00 a.m.

By the time they boarded a plane for San Antonio at five the next morning, she felt the distance between them looming like a chasm.

LUKE SAT next to Hannah on the plane, studiously avoiding any physical contact. The closer they got to Texas, the more he was sure he'd made a mistake by letting himself get involved with her in any sort of personal way. For more than one reason. He was dragging along a woman who might rat him out to her friends if she got the chance. He tried to keep that firmly in mind, even while he considered the other half of the equation—himself. His destiny lay somewhere at the end of their flight. He sensed it, and he knew that until he regained the knowledge of his background and the extent of his present problems, he had no business letting his emotions rule his relationship with Hannah or anyone else.

Unfortunately, the logic of the situation wasn't enough to turn off his feelings. Despite his doubts about her, he still craved her companionship and her comfort. But he wasn't going to let her know that. So he exercised an iron control that came from some well of inner strength that he was surprised to find existed within himself.

Keeping everything on a superficial level with his traveling companion, he followed her out of the plane, then found a rental counter where he could pick up a sport utility vehicle.

It was when they stepped outside that another kind of emotion seized him. He knew this place—in his blood and bones if not in his head.

He pulled in a draft of the air, dry and sweet with a familiar tang he couldn't quite identify. It was still early spring, but the temperature was already edging toward the nineties. And the hot sun beating on his head made him conscious that he needed a hat. So he dragged Hannah back in the building, found a phone booth and copied down some addresses.

Once they got into their rental, she sat slumped in her seat, quiet and uncommunicative as they headed away from the airport. She straightened and looked at him inquiringly when he stopped at a strip mall.

"Now what?"

"I want to get some clothes. For you, too."

He didn't give her time to argue as he climbed out of the car and waited for her to join him on the sidewalk. Inside the store, he stood looking at the racks of clothing, the hats, the boots.

Boots first. Then a hat and a shirt, he thought, something inside his chest expanding in anticipation. And then a gun. Yes, he'd definitely need one of those to replace the one he'd had to ditch before leaving for the airport in Philadelphia.

He spent forty-five minutes transforming himself from an easterner to a man at home in Western trappings.

"You need a hat and boots, too," he told her. "For the desert."

"Why?"

"There are sixteen varieties of poisonous snakes in Texas. Not to mention fire ants, scorpions and black widow spiders."

"Glad to hear it." She looked at him inquiringly. "The desert, you say. Is that where we're going?"

"Yeah," he answered, not because he knew the exact location but because the concept felt right.

He figured that if she'd come this far with him, she wasn't going to hop a plane back to Maryland. So while she was making some selections, he quietly took care of another necessary purchase, then rejoined her in the ladies' department. It amused him that she deliberately picked hiking boots over Western gear—and a hat that looked more like a souvenir of a Mexican border town rather than anything from the Lone Star State.

His next stop was a large grocery store where he picked up water, a flashlight and some emergency rations.

As Hannah looked through the purchases, she slanted him an inquiring look.

"Are we going camping?"

"We're going into territory where you might pass two cars in a hundred miles. It's best to be prepared."

"Prepared for what?"

"Disaster," he answered in a flat voice, knowing that he wasn't being ironic. He was actually expecting a disaster of some kind, although he couldn't say what.

They headed out of town, the urban scenery giving way rapidly to open spaces dotted with vegetation he recognized—mesquite, creosote bush, yuccas and century plants.

Beside him, Hannah was silent as he merged onto Route 90. But he was sure she knew his nerves were humming, the tension increasing the closer he got to Pritchard.

Mercifully, instead of engaging him in conversation, she turned on the radio, switching from country and western to south-of-the-border music when the listening areas changed.

It was a long ride. As they drove westward, the landscape grew progressively dryer, the flat plains rimmed by mountains.

When the terrain became more hilly, he sensed that they were getting close to their destination.

They arrived in Pritchard by midafternoon. It was a town that sat baking in the fierce Texas sun.

On the outskirts were ramshackle houses interspersed with house trailers. The central shopping area was a hodgepodge of buildings—some adobe, some faded wood, some brick and cinder block. But they all had one feature in common, a front porch to ward off the broiling sun.

About half the angled spaces up and down the street were filled with cars and trucks. And a number of horses were also tied up in the shade of some trees.

Pulling into a parking spot, Luke cut the engine.

"Now what?" Hannah asked.

"Coming here was your idea," he snapped, then realized he'd given too much away by the unguarded words and the way he'd spoken them.

She reached to press her small hand over his large one.

Her skin was warm and dry, a sharp contrast to his own cold, clammy flesh. He knew to the moment the last time they'd touched each other—when he'd put a new bandage on her wound. Before that had been in the car after she'd haltingly confessed her relationship with Gary Flynn. Then he hadn't been able to stop himself from reaching to comfort her. Now she was doing the same thing.

"I'm proud of you for coming here," she said.

"Did I have a choice?" he asked dismissively.

"There's always a choice." She took her upper lip between her teeth, then turned it loose to ask, "Do you remember anything?"

He shook his head. "Not on any conscious level. But as long as I'm here, I guess I should get out of the car and stroll around. See if anyone comes running to greet me or goes running in the other direction." He forced a laugh. "Maybe I'll find out I killed the mayor's grandmother, and they'll come and throw me in the clink."

"I doubt it."

They made one trip up and down the sidewalk, stopping to look at the merchandise in shop windows. Western wear. Children's clothing. Dry goods. Groceries.

After one full circuit of the business district, they were

about to start in the opposite direction again when Luke felt the hairs on the back of his neck tingle. Pretending to look at a saddle in a window, he slanted his eyes far enough to the right to see two men of Mexican extraction—one with streaks of gray in his hair—watching him intently and putting their heads together to talk. As soon as he turned fully toward them, they quickly ducked into the drugstore.

The men had recognized him. He was sure of that. And sure they didn't want to confront him directly.

As he and Hannah approached the café in the middle of the block, he heard her stomach rumble.

When he glanced at her, she blushed.

"Uh, the soft drink and crackers they served us on the plane was a long time ago," she murmured.

"Yeah. Maybe we should have a late lunch," he answered, and felt guilty when he saw her grateful look. His stomach might be too nervous for food, but she was probably starving after the long drive from San Antonio.

There were no other customers inside, and he was afraid the place might be closed. But the young, dark-skinned waitress said she'd be glad to serve them.

Luke chose a table by the window, deliberately putting himself on display to anyone who passed by. Setting his hat on the seat beside him, he picked up the menu, studying the basic Tex-Mex fare.

He figured he could handle a chicken burrito and a taco. Hannah went for the combination plate.

When the food arrived, he concentrated on getting down small bites, while Hannah tucked into her cheese enchilada.

He was halfway through his burrito when he felt the sensation of being watched again. Looking up, he saw an old Mexican woman with deeply lined skin staring at him through the glass.

Their eyes met and held. The woman's lips moved, but he couldn't understand what she was saying through the window.

Hannah must have caught the expression on his face, because she looked from him to the window.

When the woman saw them both staring at her, she took a step back, then turned and started down the line of stores. Luke leaped out of his seat, heading for the door.

He reached her before she turned the corner, then wasn't sure what to do.

"Ma'am. Uh, ma'am."

At the sound of his words she whirled, looking him up and down with dark perplexed eyes. "Maybe I made a mistake," she said in a soft voice, her speech rich with the accents of a native Spanish speaker.

"You think you know me?" Luke asked, his whole existence focused on her answer.

"Jose came running to my house saying he saw Lucas Somerville. But maybe he was mistaken…" The sentence trailed off as if she was asking him to correct the impression.

His whole body went rigid. Lucas Somerville? Was that the name he'd been born with?

He had expected—hoped and prayed—that when he heard it, memory would come back in a thunderclap of recognition. Or a great rolling wave of comprehension.

He had lots of metaphors for the phenomenon. But it turned out that none of them was worth a bucket of warm spit.

Nothing happened.

Nada.

His mind was still as blank of his personal history as it had been before he'd heard the collection of syllables.

CHAPTER NINE

Although memory still eluded him, Luke felt some sort of silent communication pass between himself and the old woman. Greedily he took in details, as if he could draw out some truth about himself by understanding her.

Her hair must have once been a rich black. Now it was streaked with silver. Her hands and feet were small, her fingers stubby. And her faded dress was a sort of shapeless sack draped over her large breasts and broad hips.

If she held out her arms, he realized with a jolt that he would go into them like a child asking for his mother's comfort. But neither of them seemed capable of movement.

"Can you tell me your name?" he asked.

"Juanita Contrares."

It had no familiarity, and again he was seized by a wave of bitter disappointment.

He was vaguely aware that Hannah had been standing behind him, listening to the exchange and holding the hat he'd forgotten on the seat beside him.

Now she spoke, explaining what he should have said himself. "Luke was in an accident. He has no memory of his past. But he picked the name Luke Pritchard for himself, and we thought that if he came here, someone might recognize him and tell him about his background."

The words made the old woman's face go slack with shock. "An accident!" she gasped, her gaze roving over his face and body.

"I'm fine," he said quickly through his parched lips. "The only problem is the gap in my memory."

Reassured, she studied him appraisingly. "You look different," she said in a thoughtful voice.

"But you think you recognize me?" he persisted.

"I worked for Señor Somerville before he died. I took care of Lucas when he was little. It's a long time since you left, but I think…I think that's who you are."

The confirmation chased some of the ice from his skin.

"You were just a boy when you left town," she went on in a stronger voice. "Your face is different. You've filled out. Matured. I don't think so many people would recognize you. But Jose worked at the ranch, too. He saw you every day."

"Why did I leave?"

"You and your father didn't get along."

Her voice was matter-of-fact, but there was a wealth of implications in the simple statement.

"I'd like to ask you more questions, Señora Contrares," Luke said, glancing around. "But not out here on the street. And not in the restaurant where other people could hear us. Is there somewhere more private where we can talk?"

She hesitated for a moment. "My home is very humble."

"Your house will be fine. Is it far? We can give you a ride."

"A ride. Sí. Thank you."

Feeling slightly disoriented, Luke led the way to the SUV, unlocked it and slipped behind the wheel. Hannah climbed in back with Juanita.

"Thank you for helping us," she said.

"Lucas Somerville was like my little boy," she said, then directed them around the corner and down several blocks.

They crossed a set of railroad tracks to an area of dirt yards, old cars and low dwellings that needed painting. Dark-haired children playing in the streets turned to look at them as they passed.

She pointed to a faded adobe, and Luke pulled up at the front walk. Inside, the furniture was old and worn, with brightly woven pieces of fabric covering what were probably holes in the upholstery. Yet everything was neat and orderly. A circulating fan in the corner stirred the hot air.

"Sit," Juanita said, looking apologetic as she gestured toward the sofa and chairs.

"You're an excellent housekeeper," Hannah said.

"I try," she answered modestly.

Luke settled onto the sofa, and Hannah sat next to him, laying her hand over his. Finding he needed the contact, he didn't pull away.

"Can I get you something? I have tea in the refrigerator."

"No, thank you. We're fine," Hannah answered.

The old woman nodded, then swung her gaze back to Luke. Her words were kindly, yet something about her appraisal made him edgy. "I hope you have had a good life since you left this town."

"I wish I knew the answer to that." He cleared his throat and decided to go for broke. "The only thing I remember is a little something about my mother."

"Carmen Luz."

Again he tried to catch some hint of recognition, but the name brought no picture to his mind.

"She left when you were seven."

"Why?"

Juanita hesitated. "It's not my place to talk about your family."

"I need to know! And it looks like you're the only one who can tell me."

She gave a small nod, considering, then began to speak in a voice that was little more than a whisper. "Your father was drinking. He used to beat her and insult her. She would talk to me about it."

"Why did she marry him?"

"He wasn't always a bad man. His family was well off. He started going to a devil's place called Las Vegas and gambling. It was like a disease with him. He lost a lot of money, and he comforted himself with drink."

"My mother came across the border illegally?"

"*Dios,* no!" the woman exclaimed, her voice dripping with indignation. "She was from a good family in Mexico. She met your father when they were both studying at the University in San Antonio. She went back to her family when she couldn't take your father's abuse any longer."

Luke's chest was so tight he could barely dredge up enough air to speak. But he had to ask the question that had been digging its claws into his mind since the session with the psychologist. "Why didn't she take me with her?"

Juanita looked sad. "Her family was proud. They had forbidden her to marry your father, but she defied them and did it anyway. And when she finally admitted to herself that they had been right all along, they allowed her to take nothing with her."

It was more than he'd hoped to hear. Perhaps she hadn't had a choice about abandoning him.

"She made me promise to take good care of you," Señora Contrares said. "And I tried my best. But your father was a hard man. Sometimes I thought he treated you like a rented mule. You were filling a man's boots before you were eight, working on the ranch with the rest of the hands." Her eyes took on a faraway look. "You grew up riding some tough mounts and making your pocket money by chasing wild horses. You were a pretty salty bronc rider, too. I think you were nine when you first came out of a bucking chute, at the Fourth of July rodeo in Marathon."

In a kind of trance, Luke listened to the recitation, unable to identify with any of the details she was handing out.

"The older you got, the more I worried that you and your father would…come to blows. Then one morning when you didn't show up at the breakfast table, I went in to see what was wrong, and you were just gone," she continued.

"How old was I?"

"Sixteen. You were tall. You looked older. You could have passed for an adult—with that mustache you wore to make yourself look older." She paused and inspected him again. "You seem like a fine man. I'm glad of that."

He gave a small shrug, then changed the subject by asking, "How long ago did my father die?"

Her vision turned inward for a moment. "Four or five years. He's buried in the graveyard behind the house. With your grandparents."

Luke took in the information without emotion, sure that he should feel something. Anything.

"Is anyone living at the ranch?"

"No. He left it to you. But you didn't come back—until now."

"To me?" he asked incredulously. "You said we hated each other."

"Maybe in the end he felt regret. I think he missed you, although he would never have said it out loud."

Luke tried to digest everything he'd heard. There were still no feelings associated with the words. It was as if the old

woman were talking about someone else. A stranger. Finally
he asked, "Can you tell me where to find the place?"

"It's on the main road out of town. About forty miles west.
It's called the Big S."

He'd run out of questions, and the room filled with silence
as the old woman swung her gaze from him to Hannah and
back again. "At least I know you have a woman who cares
about you."

He turned his head toward Hannah and saw her flush. He
might have said that she wasn't his woman. But he hadn't
come here to get into complicated explanations.

Hannah filled the sudden silence by asking, "When you
spotted Luke—Lucas—in the restaurant, you were reacting
to more than just seeing him in town."

Luke had been too busy trying to absorb the personal information to focus on anything beyond that. Now he waited
for the answer like a man on trial for murder, waiting for the
jury's verdict.

Regret flashed in Juanita's eyes. "When I saw you, I
thought the men turned out to be right."

The cryptic phrase had Luke leaning forward in his seat.
"What men? Right about what?" he demanded.

The old woman looked down at her hands, then back at
him. "I have been in this town a long time, since I came as a
girl from Mexico. People around here know me." She paused,
and made an openhanded gesture. "Jose came to tell me he
thought he saw you. And I've heard things before. Not long
ago there were rumors that someone who looked like you was
traveling around in the desert. You and some strangers nobody
recognized."

With an odd feeling of detachment, he considered the implications of her words and of the strained expression on her

face. They were near the border and in a part of the state where the wide-open spaces were vast and rugged, where traffic from Mexico was likely to skirt the law. Illegal immigration came immediately to mind. And smuggling.

"They think I was up to no good?" he asked.

She shrugged, but the evasive look in her eyes made his skin go cold and then hot. "I think maybe they don't know what you were doing."

HANNAH WATCHED Luke without training her eyes directly on him. He'd been hit with so much bad news in the past few minutes, and she suspected the temptation to simply drop this particular subject was almost overwhelming.

But she was pretty sure he was going to ask the next logical question.

"Where *exactly* was I seen?"

"I don't have the answer to that."

"Who would?" Hannah interjected.

"I can ask around," the old woman answered. "Maybe someone will be willing to talk to Lucas."

"Under the circumstances, I'm not sure it's so good for you to be seen with me," Luke said. "Or for me to be seen in town. We'd better stay somewhere else."

"What about Boylton?" Hannah asked. She'd studied the map and knew it was one of several communities within a seventy-five-mile radius of Pritchard. "Do you know the name of a motel there?"

Señora Contrares thought for a moment. "The Yucca. It's not fancy. But I know one of the maids who works there. And I know it's clean."

"Then we'll be there tonight. If you find anyone with information, send them to us there."

"*Sí.*"

Luke stood.

Juanita climbed to her feet as well. For a moment she hesitated, swaying slightly. Then she closed the distance between herself and Luke, wrapping her arms around him.

"I never thought I'd see you again," she whispered.

"I wish it were under better circumstances," he answered, returning the hug she gave him, then added in a thick voice, "I wish I remembered you."

Hannah watched them, wondering if he had clung to her like this when he'd been a little boy.

His eyes were squeezed tightly shut. Abruptly he pulled away and seemed to shake himself.

"You will get your memory back," the old woman said.

"How do you know?"

"You are a man with a strong will. You were always like that."

He made a snorting noise and turned toward the door. Hannah watched his taut shoulders as he exited through the door. She wanted to help him, but he had shut her out and there was nothing she could do about it until he decided to reverse his decision about her.

Feeling the woman's eyes on her, Hannah looked up. "This is hard for him," she murmured. "Not remembering."

"I understand. But he has you to stand by him."

"I'm a private detective. He hired me to investigate his background," she said, hastening to make the relationship clear.

"Perhaps, but I can see you care about him. And he pushes you away."

"Yes."

"Don't give up on him."

"I won't," she said, meaning it. She had learned so much

about Luke in the past half hour. Things that made her ache for the boy he'd been. Things that helped her understand his behavior. Things that fueled her admiration for him. Lord, what odds the man had overcome in his life.

Her gaze cut to the door, and she saw him sitting in the SUV, looking impatient.

"I'd better go," she said, hurrying down the walk and climbing into the passenger seat, feeling a wave of heat envelop her from the vehicle that had been baking in the sun.

Luke started the engine before she'd buckled her seat belt.

"What were you talking about?" he asked.

"I was thanking her."

"I guess I should have done a better job of that myself," he answered in a thick voice.

"I think she knew how you felt."

The conversation died again. The only time Luke spoke was when he borrowed Hannah's phone to make a reservation at the Yucca Motel in Boylton.

It didn't take long to leave the dusty town behind and head into the dry landscape that reminded her of scenes from a Western movie. There were a few stunted trees, interspersed with scraggly bushes.

"What are the trees?" she asked.

"Mesquite, mostly."

"And the bushes?"

"Creosote. Tumbleweed. Leather plant. The big spiky leaves are century plant."

"And those weird-looking tall things with the orange flowers on top?"

"Ocotillo."

"You know the names of the vegetation, but you have no specific memories of this place?"

Luke shrugged. "The scenery looks familiar. I just can't put myself into it," he said, making it clear by his tone of voice that he wanted to cut off the conversation.

She was silent for several miles, then asked, "I assume we're going to the ranch?"

"Yeah."

"To see your father's grave?"

"To see if anything jogs my memory," he answered. "Since I apparently lived there for the first sixteen years of my life."

She smoothed her finger across the textured seat cover, then finally spoke the thoughts on her mind. "I'm the one who forced you to come back here."

"It was my decision."

"Well, I thought that meeting someone from your past would trigger your memory. I'm sorry it didn't work out."

"I wasn't expecting much," he answered with elaborate casualness. Then, "You probably didn't like hearing I'd been spotted hanging around in the desert—up to no good, if you read between the lines."

"Maybe it wasn't you. Mrs. Contrares said you'd changed."

"She also recognized me. So did some guy named Jose—and his friend."

"She wasn't sure at first and she knew you pretty well."

"We can argue about that all day. The important point is that I was out there doing something on the hot side of the law."

"That's a ridiculous assumption. You might have been leading hikers into the wilderness. You might have been searching for Indian artifacts."

"Don't forget prospecting for gold," he said dryly as they rounded a curve and passed a stand of low, scrubby bushes. "I found the mother lode and converted the bullion to cash!"

She folded her arms across her chest. "Okay. Have it your way. You were smuggling drugs across the border."

"Probably."

"Stop!"

She saw his lips tighten, and he said nothing else. She knew he'd had a major disappointment today. He'd found his home, yet he still remembered nothing about his past, even after talking to the woman who had taken care of him when he was a child. He might be covering his feelings by getting into an argument, but she knew he was hurting. She wanted to reach over and touch his hand on the steering wheel. She wanted to tell him that the longer she knew him, the more sure she was that he couldn't be engaged in criminal activity. Yet she had come to understand there was no point in doing either. He didn't want her comfort or her reassurances.

So she sat silently beside him as the SUV hurtled down the highway.

In the distance she saw a vehicle slow down and stop before speeding up again.

Leaning forward, she saw orange cones blocking part of the pavement.

"What's going on up there?" she asked, flashing back to the accident scene the night before, when Luke had been afraid the police were after him.

"Border patrol," he answered in a flat voice, stepping on the brake. In light of their recent conversation, she felt her nerves jump as they slowed to a crawl. Ahead of them was a contingent of tough-looking men in stark green uniforms with pistols in black leather holsters. One of them was quizzing the driver of the truck that had been pulled over to the side. As she watched, another officer approached their vehicle with a dog on a leash who began to sniff along the underside of the vehicle.

She could see Luke's hands tighten on the wheel before he made a deliberate effort to relax.

To her relief the officer only asked if they were American citizens. When they both answered yes, he waved them through.

Hannah breathed a little sigh as they left the checkpoint behind. Silently, she tried to analyze why the men looked so intimidating. Their equipment was similar to what she'd carried as a uniformed cop in Baltimore. But their stark caps and the contrast of all that black leather against their green uniforms made them look as if they'd blow you away and ask questions later.

"Are there a lot of checkpoints?" she asked.

"Yeah. To stop illegal immigration. And smuggling."

She saw he was watching the odometer. Ten miles down the road, he slowed at a huge iron archway, the elaborate pattern making her think of when she'd been at a police convention in New Orleans. At the very top and along the side, the letter *S* was worked into the design—one facing forward and the other backward. Beyond it was a gravel road that wound into the hills.

Turning off the highway, Luke headed up the lane, his eyes fixed on a rise of land in the distance where she could see trees and a windmill spinning. After seven or eight miles, the vegetation thickened, and the trees grew taller. They drove into what would have passed for a forest in this area of the country. Coming out into a clearing, she saw a house that made her jaw drop open.

The architecture in town had been strictly utilitarian. This place was a veritable mansion in the middle of the desert. It looked as though it was made of stucco, with a tin roof and a two-story porch spanning the front, supported by Doric columns made of wood.

The first impression was of well-kept luxury. But as they

got out of the car and walked toward the structure, the blem-
ishes became more apparent. The bottoms of the porch posts
were rotting and the windows were boarded up.

"What are all these trees?" she asked.

Luke blinked. He'd been so intent on drawing some meaning from this plot of land that he'd forgotten anyone was in
the truck with him.

"Cottonwoods, crepe myrtle, pecans, figs," he answered,
then glanced back toward the spinning windmill. "It looks like
the well is still watering them."

"Do you remember the ranch?"

The brittle feeling that had followed him all the way from
town intensified. Deliberately, he looked around. To the right
of the mansion was a stretch of broken fence that had apparently once separated a complex of barns from the front yard.
The barns were in even worse shape than the house. To the
left and right, various outbuildings dotted the property. Several had collapsed into heaps of weathered boards and sec-
tions of tin roof. It was clear his father had stopped caring for
the place long before his death.

He moistened his dry lips. "No."

When Hannah started toward the house along a path
made of flat slabs of limestone, he caught up with her and
grabbed her arm.

"Don't go up there."

"Why not?"

"The boards look like they could be rotten. You don't want
to fall through into a nest of snakes."

She shuddered and gave the porch a wide berth, stopping
beside two rusted lawn chairs and a table, all fashioned from
horseshoes welded together.

Like a mortgage inspector evaluating the property, Luke

walked slowly around the side of the house, then headed for the barn. Hannah stayed a couple of paces behind him, and he hoped she wasn't going to ask any more questions he couldn't answer.

Another path behind the house led toward a little hill several hundred yards away. Staring at it, he went still. The area at the top was surrounded by a three-foot-tall iron fence and more cottonwoods. Poking up through the weeds were several gravestones, some looking as though they were about to topple over.

The graveyard. Where Lucas Somerville's ancestors were buried. Lucas Somerville.

He was supposed to be that man. He was supposed to have grown up here. But he felt no more connection to the place than he would have felt to an Alaskan igloo.

He had come here hoping for answers. Now there was only a hollow feeling in his chest as he said, "I'm going up there."

His throat was so clogged that speech was impossible. Hoping his body language made it clear that he didn't want Hannah to follow, he strode up the hill. Arriving at the fence, he hesitated for a moment, then lifted the gate that was hanging from one hinge. After stepping inside the fence, he stooped to look at one of the gravestones.

The name and the inscription were too worn to read. So he went on to the next one. The newest one.

Andrew Somerville. His father.

A hard, cold man. A drinker. A wife beater. A man who took out his anger and frustration on his son.

Luke pressed the heel of his hand against his eyes, fighting the feeling of numbness that had grabbed him by the throat. He remembered none of it. Because he didn't want to remember. That was obvious.

HANNAH WATCHED Luke's shoulders slump in defeat. Her heart squeezed and she turned away, fixing her gaze on the flower beds along the side of the house where a few ornamental plants struggled to poke their heads among the weeds.

She wanted to yank the weeds away so the struggling flowers would have the benefit of the soil and water. But she could see small cacti with wicked-looking thorns poking their heads through the other vegetation, so she kept her hands pressed to her sides.

Once more she directed a covert glance toward Luke's back, then turned quickly as a flicker of movement in the direction of the highway caught the edge of her vision.

An animal?

Shading her eyes with her hands, she was surprised to see a trail of dust kicking up through the desert. From a car or truck, she assumed.

She glanced toward Luke, but he was still in the graveyard, reaching out to straighten one of the listing tombstones.

Turning back, she watched a vehicle coming toward them along the access road. Although she couldn't make out many details, she could tell that it was some sort of light-colored big pickup, similar to scores she'd seen since arriving in Texas.

Apparently Luke had company. Did people come out here often? Was it a caretaker thinking he was dealing with trespassers? Or was it someone looking for them—someone who'd talked to Mrs. Contrares?

The guy was in a tearing hurry, and she wanted to yell at him to slow down. Still at full throttle, the vehicle disappeared from view as it reached the screen of trees, then came roaring out of the greenery. As the truck plowed through the front yard of the house, she saw that it was heading straight toward her.

Was the driver blind? She waved her arms, then realized he wasn't planning to slow down—and she had only seconds to get out of the way.

CHAPTER TEN

If she could have made it into the trees, she might have been safe. But the vehicle blocked her path.

The best she could do was sprint for the porch. Not the front, but the narrow edge on the side of the house.

There were no steps on the side, and the surface was several feet above the ground. Tearing through the flower bed, she bounded upward, thorns ripping at her jeans as she leaped onto the sagging boards. Seconds later, the truck roared over the spot where she'd been standing.

The vehicle missed her with inches to spare, shot past in a cloud of dust and made a screeching turn. Through the obscured windshield she could see a man hunched over the wheel, a cowboy hat jammed down over his face.

Breathing hard, she watched as the truck circled back, this time aiming for the SUV parked in front of the house. He rammed it from the rear, slamming the front end against the wooden porch pillar so hard that the hood crumpled.

The whole porch shuddered as Hannah fought to keep her balance, only marginally aware of what was going on around her.

In the distance she heard Luke yelling something, followed by the sound of gunshots. Did the guy have a gun, or was it Luke shooting? If he was, where had he gotten the weapon?

She'd seen him ditch his gun back in Philadelphia. That seemed like a lifetime ago…

Before she had time for further speculation, her attention was captured by another sound—the sickening crack of splintering wood. Seconds later, her foot crashed through a spongy floorboard.

God, no. Not down there with the snakes. In her vivid imagination, she heard them hissing, felt their scaly bodies slithering against her boots, then her jeans-clad legs. A scream rising in her throat, she tried to claw her way back to the surface, but the rotten wood kept breaking away in her hands.

Finally, with some desperate reserve of strength, she wrenched her foot free and flopped to the porch surface, lying prone and spreading out her arms and legs to distribute her weight.

But before she could pull herself to safety, a groan from above warned her of a new danger. A moment later, a loose section of tongue-and-groove ceiling came crashing down in a cloud of dust and debris, missing her by less than a foot.

Shaky and disoriented, she pushed herself to her knees, splinters digging into her hands as she crawled toward safety. She had almost made it to the edge of the porch when she felt the whole structure shudder and knew that disaster was imminent.

Strips of wood were raining down around her. Choking, blinded by the dust, she felt strong arms grab her by the shoulders and pull her away from the collapsing porch and into the yard. A second later, the whole roof came crashing down.

IN THE SWIRL OF DUST, Luke gathered Hannah close.

He crooned low, soothing words to her, his body curving around hers. Then a flash of movement over her shoulder caught his attention. Shifting her weight to his left arm, he grabbed his gun with his right hand and fired off two quick shots.

He felt Hannah flinch as she turned her head to see two snakes twitching on the ground. One was headless, the other was cut in two.

Her fingers clutched at Luke's forearms. "Rattlers?" she asked.

"Yeah."

Her gaze darted along the edge of the ruined porch. "Are there more?"

"There may have been. Let's assume they got crushed when their nice shady porch came crashing down."

Scooping her into his arms, he carried her to the side of the house, putting a solid wall between them and the snakes.

After moving past the flower beds, he slid downward, seating himself and shifting Hannah onto his lap as he rocked her in his arms.

Breathing hard, she clung to him. And he clung just as tightly, knowing that if he had been seconds later she would have been crushed by the collapsing roof.

For a long time, neither of them moved.

He knew she was drawing comfort from him. He knew he was doing the same thing, clinging to her because she was the only thing real and solid in the nightmare world he inhabited.

"Are you all right?" he asked, his hands stroking oh so gently across her shoulders and down her back.

"I think so." She tested the theory by shifting her arms and legs.

He saw a grimace cross her face, but nothing bad enough to indicate broken bones.

His hand went to the back of her head, gently probing the spot where she'd been injured before.

"Did it split open again?" she asked.

"It feels okay. At least that's something."

"What do you mean?"

"I mean, this is what I get for dragging you along with me," he muttered.

"No."

"What do you mean no? That guy tried to kill you!" In his mind he saw the truck again, coming straight toward her, and he swallowed painfully as he thought about the consequences if she hadn't been smart enough to get herself out of the way. "Tell me what happened," he demanded.

"I saw him on the access road. I thought he was driving too fast, that he was in a hurry to talk to you. When he came at me, I leaped onto the porch, and he rammed the SUV."

"Then he roared away," Luke finished. "I got here for the last part."

"You were shooting at him?"

"Yeah."

"I didn't even know you had a gun. When did you get it?" she asked.

"While you were buying boots and a hat."

"You can't just buy a gun like a—a box of popcorn. I thought there was a waiting period and a background check."

"Not in Texas." He was silent for several seconds, then asked, "Did you get a look at the guy in the truck? Or maybe get the license plate?"

"I was a little busy!"

"Yeah."

"But I tried. His hat was pulled down over his face. And I think the plate was smeared with dirt."

He nodded.

As he took her hand to help her up, she winced.

"What is it?" he asked.

"Splinters." She turned her palm upward so he could see.

"A couple of wicked ones, it looks like," he said. "I'd better dig them out before you get an infection."

He jogged back to the SUV, rummaged in one of the bags and came back with a first-aid kit and one of the water bottles.

"You'd better sit down and hold still."

After they'd both made themselves comfortable, he washed the dirt off her hands and his. Then he swabbed her skin with antiseptic and did the same with a needle.

Cradling her right hand in his left, he began to probe for one of the splinters. When she sucked in a sharp breath, he stopped abruptly.

"Sorry."

"There isn't any other way," she replied, nodding.

He bent to the task again, keeping his eyes focused downward because that was the only way he could keep working. He saw her grit her teeth, saw her struggle not to show him the pain he was inflicting and tried to keep his own face blank. After digging out the end of the first splinter, he used his fingernails to pull it free.

"You did fine," he murmured, then went to work on the other, which wasn't as deep. When he pulled the remaining sliver of wood from her hand, she breathed a small sigh.

"Thank you," she whispered.

"Sorry I had to hurt you," he said, the sound of his voice thick and low. Gently he stroked his thumb across her palm.

There was a moment of silence when he sensed she was waiting for him to say something more. But he felt as if he'd already given too much away. He didn't want her to think he needed her, or that he was vulnerable to her. Not now. Not here.

So he turned away and mechanically repacked the first-aid

kit, then went back to the SUV and slid behind the wheel. A few tries at the starter had him cursing. It looked as if the vehicle wasn't going anywhere under its own power.

He saw Hannah pull her cell phone from her purse and try to make a call. But either she wasn't hooked into the right network in southwest Texas, or there were no cells in this patch of wilderness.

Shoving the phone back into her bag, she craned her head in the direction of the highway. There was nothing to see but desert landscape. "I guess we could walk to the road," she suggested gamely.

He shook his head. "It would be dark before we got there, and rattlers are most active at night. I think we're better off staying put until morning."

He watched her considering the advice, weighing one danger against another. "What if the guy in the truck comes back?"

"You notice he turned tail and ran when I took a shot at him. He won't come back because he knows if he gets close enough to me, I'll drill him."

Before she could ask him another question, he looked around at the lengthening shadows and said, "We've got a lot to do before it gets dark."

First they retrieved their supplies and luggage from the truck. After setting everything down by the back door, he tried the knob. As he suspected, the door was locked.

He'd wanted to avoid going into the house, since he assumed it was only going to be another painful exercise in frustration. But he had no choice. So he lifted his foot and gave the door a swift kick. The lock snapped, and the door flew inward.

"I guess there's nothing wrong with breaking into your own property," he observed dryly as they stepped into a large kitchen with outdated appliances and linoleum counters edged with metal strips.

The air inside was dry and musty as they made their way into a dining room, then directly into a sitting room where the bulky furniture was covered with white sheets.

"Do you remember the place?" she asked, her voice no louder than a whisper.

"Not a damn thing," he answered, keeping any emotion out of his voice.

After surveying several areas, he returned to a small room at the back of the house. It appeared to be a den, with a leather couch, a desk, a fireplace and a Native American rug still on the wood floor. On the desk was a metal lamp decorated with two animal horns.

Focusing on the tasks that needed doing, he returned to the kitchen and retrieved a broom, sweeping it along the walls and edges of the ceiling.

"Getting rid of the dust?" Hannah asked.

"No. Texas is full of nasty critters you wouldn't want to cozy up with. I'm making sure there are no black widow spiders or scorpions before we camp here for the night."

She shuddered, then whipped the sheet off the couch. They both coughed when dust rose.

As she gingerly inspected the cushions, he pulled up the rug, swept the floor and threw the covering back down. Then he turned over the dusty sheet and laid it on top of the rug.

"At least we can build a fire," she said, gesturing toward the hearth.

"Not a good idea. That would be an advertisement that we're in the house."

"Right. I guess I wasn't thinking about that," Hannah acknowledged. Luke might have a memory impairment, but he was functioning on a much more efficient level than she. At least with regard to making this place as safe and comfortable as possible.

She was pretty sure that on a personal level, he wasn't doing too well. And that he wouldn't welcome any comments about his emotional state.

"I should thank you for coming prepared," she said as he brought the supplies into the room.

"There's stuff I wish I'd bought," he answered.

"We could do worse." She cleared her throat. "Although I would like directions to the bathroom."

"You mean the grove of trees out front?"

"Right," she said with a groan.

He dug a small packet of tissues out of one of the supply boxes and matter-of-factly handed it to her.

Hoping the dim light hid the color that had sprung into her cheeks, she accepted the tissues from him and shoved them into her purse.

When he escorted her back outside, it was getting dark and the temperature was dropping rapidly. Wishing she'd brought a jacket, she watched Luke inspect the underbrush with the flashlight.

"No nasty critters I can see," he said cheerfully.

"Glad to hear it," she answered, striving to match his tone.

He left her alone in the thicket, and she felt vulnerable and exposed in the growing darkness as she lowered the zipper on her jeans.

When she'd finished with the awkward procedure, she made her way toward the house, then handed off the light to Luke and waited just outside the back door.

The sun had dipped below the horizon. In the chill air, she wrapped her arms around her shoulders as she looked up at the almost full moon and the stars that were starting to fill the sky. In a half hour she suspected the heavenly show would be spectacular. But she didn't plan on being out here to look at it.

When Luke returned, he shined the flashlight beam into the cabinets and drawers, taking out several spoons and an empty soda bottle. Wondering what he had in mind, she watched him pull a length of string out of his pocket and tie the spoons around the mouth of the bottle. Then he fastened the whole thing to the inside doorknob. When he closed the door, the spoons rattled against the bottle—a very effective burglar alarm.

"Good idea," she said.

Luke tied the door closed with a piece of rope hooked to a nail sticking out of the wall. Then he lighted their way back through the house to the far end of the living room, where he turned to one of the windows and wrenched up the sash. With the glass out of the way, he partially loosened the boards that had been nailed into place over the opening.

Apparently satisfied that they could get out quickly if necessary, he ushered her into the den.

Hannah lowered herself to the sheet, propping her back against the bottom of the sofa.

Luke joined her, setting his gun down on the floor, then began rummaging in the boxes. Pushing aside a tire iron, he brought out a couple of bottles of water, then a few packages of food.

"Nothing very luxurious," he apologized as he laid out paper-towel squares on which he set peanut butter crackers, apples and canned meat.

Picking up a cracker, she tried a small conversational gambit. "I used to love these when I was a kid."

"Um-hum."

In the dark, she could only imagine the neutral expression on his face. Figuring that she couldn't get less of a response, she switched topics as she tried a bite of the canned meat.

"Who do you think came after me in that truck?"

"Someone with a grudge against me. Or a grudge against my family. Or someone who lost a million dollars and figures I have it."

"But if he kills you, he'll never get his money."

"He wasn't trying to kill me. He was trying to kill you."

At his blunt statement, the meat she had just swallowed turned to lead in her stomach. "Why?" she finally managed to say. "He doesn't even know me."

"A warning, maybe. That I'd better cough up the money."

She came back instantly with a second opinion. "Or a random act of terror. He saw us drive up here, knew this place was isolated, and figured he could get his jollies, get away with anything he wanted."

"So it was just a coincidence? Like the guys who arrived at the town house?"

"That wasn't a coincidence. Somebody traced you there."

She waited in the darkness, hoping he would tell her he'd realized she didn't have anything to do with the attack. When he didn't answer, she forced herself to chew another cracker, washing it down with several swallows of water.

It was almost a relief when he finally said, "We should switch off the flashlight. And you should try to get some sleep."

"What about you?"

"Somebody's got to stand guard."

"I thought you said the guy who tried to run me down wouldn't come back here."

"I don't think he will. I'm not going to bet my life on it, though. And there are other possibilities. Pritchard is a small town. By now a lot of people know I've talked to Juanita and figured out that I might have come out here."

"That's probably right, but you can't stay up all night. Wake me so I can take a shift."

"Okay," he agreed, but she wasn't sure if he intended to do it.

He switched off the light, and she stretched out on the sheet-covered rug, using her carry bag as a pillow.

A blanket would have been nice, too, but she could only dream of such niceties.

She slid her eyes toward Luke. After he'd rescued her from the porch, he'd held her in his arms and she'd felt as if all the mistrust and the bad feelings of the past twenty-four hours had been wiped away. But gradually the feeling of closeness had eroded. Now there were so many things she wanted to say. But he'd made it difficult for her to communicate on any kind of meaningful level, so she simply rolled to her side and lay there in the darkness.

ADDISON JENNINGS STOOD on the darkened patio of the manor house that headquartered the Peregrine Connection, staring out at the night sky. In Washington, D.C., sixty miles to the north, the ambient light dimmed the radiance of the night sky, but out here in the country, the heavens were filled with stars. Not as many as when he'd been on assignment in Peru or San Marcos. But enough to make him feel like a tiny speck of dust against the vastness of the universe.

It was still early spring, and the Virginia night was chilly, but he'd come out here hoping the cold air would clear his troubled mind.

Hearing footsteps behind him, he turned and was surprised

to find Connie standing in the doorway. Apparently she'd been as restless as he.

The light from the doorway made it impossible to see her face. But as soon as she spoke, his senses went on alert.

"There's been a development in Baltimore. Sedgwick's men raided a town house in the Canton area."

"Was anyone killed?"

"Not as far as our intelligence reports. A car was stolen several blocks away."

They had both stepped back into the lighted office, both taken their accustomed seats—Addison behind his wide desk and Connie on the other side.

"Were they after Reese?" he asked.

"I don't know. Maybe—" She stopped, a look of indecision coming into her eyes.

"What?" he commanded sharply.

"I don't want to get your hopes up. But maybe our operative isn't dead after all."

LUKE LAY in the darkness, listening to the gentle breathing of the woman next to him. Her scent and the heat from her body were driving him crazy. But he wasn't planning to reach for her—for a whole host of reasons.

In an effort to cool himself down, he deliberately turned to his speculations about her motives. Maybe she'd been careless about revealing the location of his town house. Maybe the money was too much of a temptation and she'd been willing to split the cash with her friends. Or maybe she was totally innocent, and whoever was looking for him had somehow traced him to Baltimore. If that were true, he'd like to know what clues he'd inadvertently dropped, what factor he'd overlooked. Or did he have some connection to the city that he didn't remember?

He didn't know. And the frustration made him clench his fists. Sternly he ordered himself to relax. He had a long day ahead tomorrow. And tonight he had to at least rest.

Yet relaxation was impossible. His awareness of Hannah would have been enough to keep him awake. But she wasn't the only factor. Everything that had happened today pressed down on his chest with a weight he could hardly bear.

He'd driven to Pritchard, Texas, with a hard knot of apprehension making his stomach ache. And when he'd finally gotten to town, the letdown had been almost more than he could bear. He'd expected to feel something. Find out something. Discover the key to his past life. Instead, there had been a blazing flash of nothing.

Nothing at all.

No memories. No impressions. No hopes.

Just the eternal blankness that had enveloped him for weeks.

Not even meeting the woman who said she'd raised him had made any damn difference. Or seeing his father's gravestone.

Andrew Somerville. It meant nothing to him. Like his own name. Lucas Somerville.

He whispered it aloud, trying to get some meaning from the syllables. But he might as well have been reciting a name he'd copied from one of the gravestones up on the hill. It sounded less familiar than Luke Pritchard.

He squeezed his eyes closed, then opened them again, staring into the darkness of the house where he was supposed to have grown up, for Lord's sake. But being here did nothing for him. Like the town, it was unfamiliar.

Well, not completely unfamiliar. He didn't remember the people or the events of his own life. But he knew the names of the plants. The tang of the desert air teased his senses. He knew how to combat the natural dangers of the area—the snakes, the scorpions, the black widow spiders.

Selective amnesia, he thought with a snort. Was his mind protecting him from the past?

He knew from Juanita that his childhood had been bad. And his life over the past few years? It looked as if he was hiding from that as well.

It was chillier in the room than it had been several hours earlier. Beside him, Hannah stirred. He lay rigid on the makeshift bed as she rolled toward him in the darkness, draping her arm intimately over his chest.

"Hannah?"

The rhythm of her breathing didn't change. She was still asleep. He shifted ever so slightly so that he could slip his own arm around her shoulder, the movement pressing her breast against his ribs. Another considerable distraction.

The temptation to focus on his pleasurable response to the woman lying next to him rather than on the painful hole in his memory was overwhelming. There was not a scrap of light in the room, and he couldn't see her. But he had a perfect image of her sable hair, her silk skin, her pretty lips.

In the darkness, he moved his hand upward to gently stroke his fingertips against the blunt ends of her hair.

Her arm moved, shifting across the fly of his jeans, and he cursed silently at the sexual jolt that shot through him.

He wanted to pull her body on top of his, feel the pressure of her breasts against his chest, cradle his erection against the cleft at the top of her legs. He contented himself with turning his face and stroking his lips against her hair.

He knew the moment she woke, the moment she became aware of her arm resting against the shaft of rigid flesh he couldn't hide.

CHAPTER ELEVEN

When Hannah started to pull away, it was impossible to simply let her go. Luke's arm seemed to have a will of its own as it tightened around her shoulder.

A while ago he had been wondering whether he could trust her. Now his suspicions seemed as insubstantial as the cobwebs he'd swept out of the room. Against his better judgment, he whispered, "Stay here."

The stiffness went out of her as she did what he asked. Her only concession to propriety was that she raised her arm a little higher so that it was now across his abdomen. He longed to snatch it back, to retain the pressure of her flesh against the part of him that ached for her, but he restrained himself.

When she started to speak, it took several seconds before he realized what she was saying.

"I'm sorry."

"About what?"

"Plastering myself to you."

He felt a hitch in his throat. "It's cold. You were trying to get warm, and I like holding you."

"Do you?" she asked, her voice turning breathy.

"Darlin', you know I do."

He closed his eyes as he felt her hand creep upward, flatten against his chest, over his heart and he knew the accelerated beat gave another indication of just how much he was enjoying having her in his arms, in his bed, even if it was only a makeshift pallet on the floor.

He told himself that carrying this interlude any further was a mistake. Still, he found his own hand mirroring her action; only when he touched her chest, his fingers gently curved around her breast.

Her little indrawn breath rippled through his whole body. And once he'd touched her, it was so natural to move his fingers, find the tight bead of her nipple, stroke back and forth across that tantalizing nub of flesh.

She didn't move. But her breath turned fast and shaky.

After a few moments of silence, she asked in a voice that broke in the middle of the sentence, "What are we doing?"

"Giving in to temptation. But only so far."

"Why only so far?"

His hand moved from her breast, up the slender column of her neck to her cheek. "You know, I'd hate for us to get killed because I'd gotten so wound up in what we were doing that the guy with the truck came sneaking back and I didn't even know he was here."

She sighed, just a little sigh, but the sound tore at him.

Before he thought about what he was doing, he reached for her and did what he'd been fantasizing about. Pulling her up, he settled her so that her body was draped intimately on top of his.

Even with the layers of clothing between them, they both reacted to the potency of the position.

It felt good. Sinfully good.

He wanted to cup his hands around her head, bring her mouth to his for a long, deep kiss. But if he did, he knew he'd drive every other thought from his mind. And it would be unforgivable not to keep her safe—since he was the one who had dragged her along on his Texas quest.

Silently she lowered her head and pressed her cheek against his shoulder.

As his hands soothed across her back, he wondered if he'd ever wanted a woman as much as he wanted Hannah.

She stirred against him.

"Better lie still, darlin'," he cautioned.

"Or what?"

"Or I'll stop being able to stand guard. And there's no point in telling me you don't care about that, because it's non-negotiable."

She made a small sound and shifted off him, coming down heavily on the sheet beside him, her breath jagged, and he was instantly angry with himself. He'd been hot and needy—and he'd deliberately gotten her into the same state.

Well, there was surely something he could do about that. Rolling to his side, he leaned over and found her mouth in the dark, his lips and tongue playing games with hers while his hands found the front of her T-shirt. He cupped her breasts through the fabric, reveling in her response.

Silently, without asking permission, he pushed the fabric up, caressing her now through the thin barrier of her bra, teasing her until she was moaning and straining upward against his fingers.

His head spun. He wanted her naked. He wanted to see her. See the look of arousal that he knew had altered her features. And see the arousal of her body—the tight peaks crowning her breasts, the flush of her skin. More than anything, he wished they were in a comfortable bed, with soft lamplight to illuminate her face.

He stroked his lips over her cheek, found her ear, and

nibbled at the tender flesh, drawing a sound of pleasure from deep in her throat.

But when he started to drag her bra out of the way, she stopped him with her hand.

"Luke, you said you wouldn't…give up on guard duty, so where are we going with this?" she managed to say between gulping breaths of air.

He went very still. "What do you mean where are we going? Where do you think we're going?"

She reached up to touch his face, stroking her fingers across his cheek. "I think you're planning something…chivalrous."

There was no point in denying his intentions. "Is that so bad?"

Her answer came back fast and low. "You're thinking about my relationship with Gary. You're thinking I need an outlet for my tension, so you're providing some…stimulation."

His response to that bit of nonsense was explosive. "Hell! You've got *that* part figured dead wrong."

"Then what's going on?"

He didn't want to explain his motives, yet he couldn't leave her with the wrong assumption she'd made. "Okay, here's how it was," he growled. "I was lying here burning up with wanting you. Then you woke up, and I couldn't keep my hands off you. I figured the best way to make amends was to…do the right thing by you."

For long moments she said nothing, and he wondered how the confession had come across. Then she reached down to knit her fingers with his.

They lay together in the darkness, their linked hands the only point of contact.

"You wanted me?" she asked.

"Wasn't that pretty obvious?" It was still obvious, but he didn't think it would be smart to prove the point.

"And in the morning you're going to pretend none of this happened." It was a statement, not a question.

"That's a good plan."

For long moments she didn't answer. Then she cleared her throat. "As long as we've agreed that we're going to forget about this conversation in the morning, we might as well discuss your other big reason for backing off. You don't trust me. Although that really shouldn't stop you from taking what I'm offering you. You can just consider it a pleasurable experience—then walk away when you're ready."

Was that what he wanted to do? He didn't honestly know. He'd hired her because of some deeply buried longing that he hadn't been man enough to acknowledge. Then, after the raid at the town house, he'd compensated by swinging completely in the opposite direction.

Instead of examining his motives out loud, he said, "I'm not in a position to trust anything or anyone. Not until I figure out where I got that suitcase full of money—and who has it in for me in Pritchard, Texas. So consider it a favor that I'm not putting any demands on you."

She made a sound of protest, although he knew she had to be smart enough to understand what he was saying.

"I'm on your side," she murmured.

He longed to believe her. And even if he couldn't, he wanted to gather her close, press her body to his once more. But he knew starting up again was a bad idea. So he rolled to his side, his back to her, hoping he was giving her a chance to get back to sleep.

DALLAS SEDGWICK HAD always thought of himself as a fair man—within the boundaries of behavior he'd learned from childhood. Which was why Chad Crosby was still alive. It wasn't Crosby's fault that the raiding party had gotten to Baltimore a few minutes too late.

So Dallas had contained the impulse to strike out. In fact, he was giving his assistant the chance to make things right—the chance within the next few days to find the man using the name Luke Pritchard.

Crosby didn't know he had a deadline, of course. He need never know—unless he failed again. Then he'd understand the price for inefficiency.

Meanwhile, they *had* come up with a piece of very interesting information. Pritchard had a traveling companion. An attractive young woman.

Was she working with him? Or was she some kind of hostage? Either way, she could make it easier to find their quarry, since two made for an easier target than a solitary gunman. Hopefully, she'd also make it easier to handle the man when they caught up with him, since he might not want to see his lady friend tortured and murdered.

HANNAH LAY beside Luke, wanting to reach out and touch him, convince him that he was wrong about himself—and about her.

But she knew that at least one of the things he'd said was right. They were in a dangerous situation and somebody had to worry about the guy with the truck.

Still, it was impossible to ignore the feelings he'd generated, or the things he'd said. He'd told her he wanted her and that it was his fault both of them were lying here hot and needy.

She longed to do something about that. But she wasn't planning to make things worse for either of them. So she forced herself to ignore the sensation of blood rushing hotly in her veins and pooling in certain areas of her body.

Somehow, she drifted into an uneasy sleep. She woke abruptly some time later to see gray light filtering in through the cracks in the boards that covered the window. Luke was crouched over her, the gun in his hand, and for a startled moment she had no idea what was going on.

God, had he come to the conclusion that she was the enemy?

Her body tensed. Then she heard a far-off rattling noise and realized it was his early-warning system—the cutlery clanging against the bottle he'd hung from the doorknob.

"Stay here," he ordered, springing up and whirling toward the door.

Before she could protest he had disappeared into the next room. In the dim light she moved toward the boxes he'd left on the floor and found the tire iron. Wishing he'd obtained two firearms instead of one, she wrapped her fist around the cold metal, straining her ears, listening for sounds of a scuffle from the front of the house. She heard nothing, but she couldn't just wait here. What if something had happened to Luke? What if he needed her help?

Glancing at her watch, she saw that it wasn't quite seven in the morning. Cautiously, she tiptoed out of the den and into the living room, staying close to the wall, the tire iron held at the ready.

A shaft of light pierced the darkness, and she stopped. Then she realized it was coming from the window where Luke had loosened the boards last night. The window was raised and the boards were gone.

Again she hesitated. But she'd already come this far, so she moved along the wall, then cautiously peered out.

A truck was parked down by the barn, and she immediately felt a shiver of reaction—until she realized it wasn't the same vehicle. The one last night had been light-colored. This one was dark.

She saw no one outside. As quietly as possible, she slipped her leg through the window, easing her body over the sill, then sliding to the ground where she stood blinking in the watery morning sunlight.

Holding her weapon in front of her, she moved along the outside wall, toward the back of the house.

When she saw a man's broad back and dark hair, she hefted her weapon, then realized it was Luke—and that he was holding his gun on another man who stood with arms raised, his fingertips trembling.

"Please, Señor Somerville, don't shoot me!"

"Give me a reason why not."

The harsh words made Hannah realize she'd created a dangerous situation. If Luke heard her and whirled around, that would give the other guy a chance to take him.

"Luke, I'm behind you," she called out, moving forward when she knew he'd gotten the message.

The other guy was small and wiry, with a dark complexion and eyes as dark as Luke's. He wore a T-shirt, jeans, boots and a straw cowboy hat. He stood with his hands raised, flicking his eyes to her, then back to the gun Luke had leveled at his belly.

"What are you doing here?" she asked.

"Juanita sent me," he answered in thickly accented English. Apparently Spanish was his native language.

"Oh, yeah," Luke retorted. "Well, Juanita doesn't know we're here."

"Last night she told me you would be at the Yucca Motel in Boylton," the man said. "I went there early, and they said you never showed up. So I figured you might have come to the ranch."

"How convenient," Luke answered.

"Can I put my hands down, *señor?*"

"Convince me I can trust you."

The man was struggling to project sincerity, Hannah thought as she watched his face. She'd seen that look on collars she'd apprehended. It meant that they desperately wanted you to know they were telling the truth—but it was no guarantee that they actually were. Because Honest John could turn around and knife you in the back if you weren't careful.

"Juanita is my cousin," the man continued. "She said you were asking for information."

"And your name is…?"

"Diego Cortez."

"You and a million other guys," Luke muttered.

"You want to know who saw you in the desert. And where."

"And you know?"

"Maybe it wasn't you," the man hedged.

"Where was this alleged sighting?"

"Just this side of Big Bend. In the mountains."

"Be a tad more specific."

"Off the West River Road. Near Buenos Aires."

"And who was it that saw me?"

"Men from town. Men who remember you."

"You got some names?"

The man shook his head. "Sorry, *señor.*"

Hannah wondered if Luke knew the location Cortez had mentioned, but she kept the question locked inside her because she didn't want to give the other guy any more information. Realizing she still held the tire iron like a club, she lowered her arm so that the weapon dangled by her leg.

"The West Road near Buenos Aires covers a lot of territory," Luke said. "It's wide-open country."

"I came prepared," Diego was saying. "I have drawn a map to show the place for you."

"What am I going to find there?"

The man shrugged. "I don't know. You are the one who said you wanted to go there."

When Luke nodded, Diego continued, "The map is in my pocket. If I reach in my pocket, do not shoot me."

"Go ahead," Luke told him, although he didn't lower his own weapon.

Carefully Cortez slid his hand into his pocket and pulled out a folded piece of paper. It was a section of a printed map, with additional lines drawn on it. Extending his hand, he gave the paper to Luke.

"I can take the gun," Hannah said, moving up beside him.

"No, that's okay."

Luke engaged the safety, then slipped the weapon into the waistband of his jeans.

She saw Diego's shoulders relax.

Luke bent to the map, studying the markings, then he looked up. "You have any idea about what's going on out there?"

Diego shrugged. "I stay out of other people's business. It's safer."

"But you came looking for us."

"Because Juanita asked me to speak to you."

Luke nodded. "We also need a favor. A ride back into town."

"I can do that. Yes. I saw your truck was damaged."

"Somebody followed us out to the ranch yesterday afternoon and made sure that we couldn't leave."

"You know who did it?"

"I'll find out," Luke answered, his mouth hardening. Instructing Diego to wait outside, he led Hannah back into the house.

"You trust that guy?" she asked once they were alone.

"Only so far. He could be leading us on a wild-goose chase—or into an ambush."

"What would be his motivation?"

"I wish I knew."

Hannah shared his frustration but didn't see any point in voicing her concern.

Quickly they gathered up their supplies and luggage and left the house. When they rejoined Diego, he was already waiting behind the wheel of his truck.

The vehicle had a king cab. Luke climbed in the back, leaving the front passenger seat for Hannah, who kept her eyes peeled for the truck that had tried to run her down the afternoon before.

"We might as well keep our motel reservation in Boylton," Luke said as they came to a desert crossroads. "Unless they gave the room away."

"It was still vacant when I went looking for you this morning," Diego answered.

"So how did you say you were related to Juanita?" Luke asked, his voice thickening to a slow, friendly drawl as they headed away from the ranch.

Diego launched into a long explanation of complicated relationships that left Hannah's head spinning.

When the man had finished, Luke had other friendly questions—about Diego's family and what he did for a living. By the time they reached the outskirts of Boylton, you would never have known that an hour earlier, Luke had been holding a gun on the other man.

He got the key from the office, promising to vacate by 11:00 a.m. checkout time or pay for an extra day. Then he asked Diego, "Is there somewhere in town where I can rent a truck or an SUV?"

"If you mean a rental company, no. But I can introduce you around. If you can pay, someone will lend you his truck," Diego offered.

"Appreciate it."

They agreed that Hannah would get cleaned up while Luke went to take care of the transportation.

She was towel-drying her hair when he came back looking annoyed.

"Problems?" she asked.

"I think we've got an SUV, but it belongs to a guy named Manuel who doesn't have a phone. Diego is driving out there. He'll come back with Manuel to give him a ride."

"That's our only option?"

"I could beat the bushes on my own. But I don't know how far I'd get."

"You think he's stalling us?" she asked.

"I wish I knew." Luke grabbed clean clothing and headed into the bathroom. Then they had a Western breakfast of steak and eggs at the coffee shop next door to the motel. But it was obvious Luke's mind was more on their transportation than on the meal because he kept glancing out the window every few seconds.

HANNAH WAS WATCHING Luke restlessly pacing back and forth in front of the motel-room window when a green SUV pulled into the parking area.

The man with the truck apparently spoke little English, so the negotiations were conducted mostly in Spanish. Still, Hannah was pretty sure Luke had paid an exorbitant price to use the vehicle for a couple of days.

After the men left, he went to pick up a few more supplies, and when he returned, they loaded their belongings into the cargo area. The gun went into the door pocket—within easy reach—along with several spare magazines.

The temperature had been fairly cool early in the morning. Now it was nearly eleven and Hannah could feel the heat building. She was grateful for the air-conditioning as they headed southwest into a landscape that was much like the day before, only the vegetation was lower and more sparse as the flat land gave way to hillier country with craggy reddish-brown mountains in the background. Above them, the sky was incredibly blue and streaked with a few wispy clouds.

Luke consulted the map Diego had given him, turning off the two-lane highway onto a gravel road.

Within ten minutes, they had left all signs of civilization behind, and Hannah knew that this was country where getting lost or having your car break down might mean dying of thirst.

As they bounced across a wide stretch of dry riverbed, she slanted Luke a considering look. "Do you remember this area?"

"I don't know." He stopped speaking abruptly as he negotiated the rocky surface, and she thought he wasn't going to say anything more. Then he surprised her by adding, "Driving through here makes me feel like something's going to happen."

"Or something *did* happen," she suggested.

He nodded tightly, but as they penetrated farther into the desolate landscape, she saw that Luke was carefully studying every outcropping of rock and small hill, as well as the road.

"Are you looking for a good place to stage an ambush?" she asked, keeping her voice as even as possible.

"Yeah."

They came to a spot where another gravel road came out of nowhere and crossed their route. Luke stopped and consulted the map Diego had given him, his eyes narrowing.

"What's wrong?" Hannah asked.

"I'd swear we've just taken the long way around."

"I guess he doesn't know this country as well as he thought," Hannah said, as much to assuage her own feeling of uneasiness as anything else.

Her attention was diverted as they crested a hill. Below them on the other side, she could see a low area much greener than the dry hills.

"I guess there's water down there," she said, expecting a creek of some kind.

"That's the floodplain along the Rio Grande."

She stared, trying to spot the water. But from where they sat, it was completely hidden.

"Where's the river? I mean, I expected something memorable."

"It's not very wide along here. But you can catch a glimpse of it if you watch."

She focused her eyes on the greenery, then felt the SUV slow as they came around another curve.

Luke glanced up at a ruined adobe that commanded a rugged promontory above the road. The roof of the building was missing, along with large chunks of adobe blocks.

Then a glint of metal flashed at one of the windows. Slamming his foot on the brake, Luke threw the vehicle into Reverse just as the crack of a rifle sounded and a bullet glanced off the roof of the SUV.

CHAPTER TWELVE

Luke brought the truck to a bouncing halt behind an outcropping of rock. More bullets pinged around them, sending a shower of stone chips into the air.

Hannah couldn't see who was shooting at them. But she knew where the shots were coming from—the adobe house high on the hill above them.

"Come on. We've got to get out of the truck." Before the engine ground to a shuddering halt, Luke opened the driver's door.

Hannah ripped off her seat belt, jouncing forward and catching herself against the dashboard as the vehicle bucked like a bronco with a burr under its saddle.

Luke's hand was on her arm, steadying her. First he grabbed the gun and the spare clips he'd stuffed into the door pocket. Then he was guiding her across the seat as he eased out of the vehicle, taking her with him. Hot desert air slapped her in the face as she stumbled to the dusty ground. When something thorny dug through the knee of her jeans, she gave a little cry.

His head whipped toward her, and she saw the jolt of fear in his eyes. "I'm not hit. I just got a couple of cactus thorns in the knee," she reassured him.

He clamped her arm, guiding her away from the truck. She didn't waste any breath asking where they were going. This

was Luke's home ground. Even if he didn't remember who
he was, he'd proven over and over again that he knew the territory and knew what he was doing.

More shots rang out, echoing off the rocks and sending
more chips into the air, too close for comfort.

Ducking, Hannah let Luke lead the way around another
sandstone formation, putting a solid barrier between them and
the shooter—or shooters. She was pretty sure it was more than
one guy up in that adobe.

The assumption was confirmed as she heard more shots.
Now that she wasn't so focused on getting out of the line of
fire, she could hear two distinct weapons.

The guys up there should be saving their ammunition, she
thought with professional detachment.

"Do you think they're coming down?" she asked Luke.

"Not if we convince them they'll get blown away." He
glanced in the direction from which the gunfire had come. "I
guess we know why Diego sent us the long way around—and
why it took so long to get the vehicle in the first place. He
wanted to give the guys up there time to set things up."

"Or somebody else knows what he told us and hustled out
here to take advantage of his directions."

"That's possible," he conceded. "Either way, we're in a
tight spot again." He was holding the pistol he'd taken from
the door pocket. From his waistband, he pulled out an almost
identical weapon and handed it to her along with two spare
clips of ammunition.

"Where did you get that?"

"In town, when I went for more supplies."

She accepted the gun and hefted the weight in her hand,
conscious that she hadn't fired a weapon since the night Sean
Naylor had been killed.

LUKE WATCHED her face. She was scared, but she was handling it. The way she handled everything, including the abuse he'd heaped on her.

He'd known it was risky coming out here in the desert. But he'd come anyway—to find out the truth about himself, because it appeared that was the only way he was going to do it.

The decision made sense for him. But there hadn't been any need to drag Hannah along—except for the rationalization that he couldn't trust her out of his sight.

He cut off that thought. There wasn't time for the luxury of self-recrimination. Instead, he said, "This is what we're going to do. You'll draw their fire. So while I circle around the back of their eagle's nest and get into position behind them, fire off a few shots in their direction every so often." As he spoke, he removed his own Stetson and placed it on her head. She had to push it back to keep it from falling over her eyes.

He could see from her expression that she didn't want him to leave her out here in the desert with the sun beating down on her and two armed men on the hill above her.

In truth, it made his stomach clench to think about abandoning her. Because the plan he'd hatched could backfire on him if the shooters got cocky and thought they could come down here and take them.

But the alternative was crouching here in the broiling sun waiting for the shooters in the adobe to get tired of sitting tight. Or worse, for reinforcements to arrive.

"Can you handle that?"

"Yes," she answered in a thin voice. Then, more strongly, "How long will it take you to get into position?"

He thought for a minute, wavering between an overly cautious appraisal or giving too long an estimate, which could take her by surprise. "I might make it in thirty minutes. But don't worry if it takes longer."

"Okay."

He gave her a quick fierce hug, and she clung to him as though they might not see each other again. Before he could talk himself into a change of plans, he turned and crouched low, making a wide circle around the hill where the gunmen perched, thorns and prickly vegetation clawing at his pant legs as he moved through the underbrush.

HANNAH PRESSED into the shade, feeling as if her mind had gone into free fall. Taking off Luke's hat, she cradled it in her arms, hugging it against her chest and rubbing her face against the crown as she stared at the sun-drenched desert spread before her. The sandy soil was studded with scrubby vegetation—yuccas, tumbleweed and the bushes Luke had called creosote. It looked like a location for an old John Wayne movie. Only this was no movie, and she was smack in the middle of the action. With a gun in her hand.

She held the hat for a few moments longer, then jammed it back on her head as she eased to the edge of the rock. Staying under cover, she fired off a couple of shots in the direction of the adobe, then ducked back around the rock.

The fire was rapidly returned. So she knew the guys were still up there, still thinking that Luke was pinned down and shooting at them.

A surge of adrenaline hit her then. She'd taken a couple of shots at the bastards, and they'd fired back. She'd done it. After months of thinking she'd lost her nerve, she'd come through for Luke, given him the edge he needed. The bad guys would stay focused on the place where they thought he was hiding. They wouldn't be watching their backs or scanning the landscape. They'd keep their attention here.

Despite the grim circumstances, she grinned, then squeezed off another few rounds, pressing her back against the rocks as the answering volley came and wishing there was more she could do to help Luke. But she was in an unfamiliar environment. So she stayed where she was, holding off before firing again.

IT TOOK TWENTY hot, sweaty minutes for Luke to reach the other side of the hill, during which he wished that he'd grabbed a water bottle from the car.

He raised his head toward the hill, trying to decide on the best way up, knowing that if either of the men got an inkling that he was in back of them, he'd be a sitting duck, because he couldn't climb with a gun in his hand.

But there was no other way to get them out of their perch up there. Not unless the helicopter fairy came to his aid. In her soundless invisible helicopter.

So he began the ascent, carefully finding hand and footholds that he hoped wouldn't cause a rock slide or turn out to be the hiding place of a sleeping rattler.

The necessity for caution made the climb long and slow. When more shots echoed off the canyon walls, he cursed as he almost lost his grip on a chunk of rock. He should have been prepared for the sound. He'd told Hannah to keep the bastards busy.

Hannah. Lord, she was brave. And loyal. How could he have doubted her loyalty?

Because he had so many doubts about himself. And he'd transferred some of them to her, he supposed.

The smartest thing she could have done was turn and run

in the other direction from him. But she'd stuck like white on rice. And all he'd given her was grief.

He'd progressed another few feet when the sound of more shots from below pierced the air. They were returned by the guys at the top of the hill. Knowing Hannah was keeping the thugs busy, he scrambled farther upward, then paused just below the summit to wipe a trickle of sweat from his face. This was it—the most dangerous part of the whole deal because he could be looking right down a gun barrel.

Pushing the image aside, he raised up enough to peer cautiously over a ridge of rock. Twenty feet ahead, he could see the top wall of the adobe. Again he inched upward, giving himself a better view.

Through a gaping hole in the rear of the ruined building, he could see the backs of two men dressed in long-sleeved shirts, boots, jeans and cowboy hats. They were both facing forward, both resting their rifle barrels on the remnants of the window frames.

He hoisted himself over the edge, stood and pulled out his automatic.

"Drop your guns, then put your hands in the air," he called out.

There was a moment of shocked silence.

"Drop your weapons, then turn around," he growled. "Nice and easy."

One of the men started to obey. The other whirled, raised his rifle and squeezed off a couple of shots.

Luke danced to the side, putting a boulder between himself and the shooter. He moved around to the other side in time to see that the gunman who had originally complied was scrambling through a hole in the front wall. As far as Luke could see, he'd taken a flying leap off the edge of the cliff.

Hannah must have seen him do it, because she started shooting from below, drawing the attention of the guy who was still inside.

Luke was able to put a bullet in the man's shooting arm, and he screamed as he dropped his weapon. Sinking to the floor of the adobe, the gunman clutched his arm and began to moan.

Luke picked up the rifle and tossed it over the side of the cliff, then inspected the guy. His straight black hair was streaked with gray, and he looked to be in his mid-forties, with a lined, weathered face. On the back of the hand pressed over his wound was a tattoo of an ornate dagger.

"You a friend of Diego?" he asked.

"I'm not telling you anything," the man answered in Spanish.

"Suit yourself," Luke replied in the same language, then gestured with the gun. "We're going down."

"I can't walk."

"You don't need your arm to walk. Now get up before I fix it so you'll never walk again."

"I'll bleed to death."

Luke hardened his voice. "Not if we hurry. Now get going." He didn't like leaving the arm untreated, but he could hardly put his weapon down to do anything about it.

With a grimace, the gunman pushed himself to his feet, clutching his arm.

"We're coming down," Luke called to Hannah, his voice echoing strangely as it bounced off the rocks. "Can you hear me?"

Her reply came with the same echo. "Luke? What happened up there? Are you all right?"

"I'm fine. One of the guys took a bullet in the arm. The other got away."

"I saw him."

"Do you know where he went?"

"No."

"Well, keep an eye out for him. And shoot if you see anything moving—except us, of course."

"Okay."

She sounded fine, but he called down, "Are *you* all right?"

"Yes."

He breathed out a small sigh and thanked God for taking care of her. Then he ordered the wounded man to step toward the door of the crumbling adobe.

"What's the best way down?" he asked as they moved toward the edge of the hill.

"Over there." His captive gestured with his dagger hand toward a winding trail.

It was a much quicker climb down than up. Fifteen minutes later they reached the truck, then the rock where Hannah had been hiding.

The sun had traveled westward in the sky, providing a bit of shade from the shadows of the rock.

The wounded man was gray-faced. Pressing his back against the solid surface, he slid to a sitting position. Sweat beaded his forehead, and blood had soaked through the sleeve of his shirt.

Luke stared at him, thinking there were a number of ways to force him to talk, but not if he lost consciousness from lack of blood. "Can you keep him covered while I get the first-aid kit?"

Hannah nodded, and he started cautiously for the truck, watching to make sure that the guy's partner—or some of their other friends—didn't suddenly appear.

When he returned, the injured man was speaking haltingly to Hannah, this time in English. He stopped talking abruptly when Luke reappeared.

"He trying to con you into letting him go?"

"Yes. But he didn't get very far."

"You get any useful information?"

"I know they came out here this morning after we left town."

The man glared at her as if she'd betrayed a confidence.

"So that was after we had our encounter with Diego," Luke muttered. "Anything else?"

"He didn't expect to be in this fix."

"I'll bet." Squatting, Luke ripped away the man's sleeve, then examined his arm. "You'll live. It's a flesh wound." Working quickly, he wound a bandage around the arm, then sat back on his heels.

"Now you're going to tell me who sent you out here to ambush us," he said in a conversational tone.

"No."

"You have a lot of loyalty. But it's misplaced."

"Please, Señor Somerville, I have to live around here. You can leave anytime you want. You did leave. You should never have come back."

The use of his real name made Luke's throat tighten. He wanted to ask the man point-blank if they'd met before. But he wasn't willing to give that much away. Instead, he offered, "Maybe I can arrange transportation to somewhere else."

The man eyed him with a spark of interest. "You would do that for me?"

"If you cooperate."

"Cooperating would be dangerous for me."

Again, a question hovered on Luke's lips, but he kept from speaking it as he looked down at their captive. He almost felt sorry for the poor bastard. Apparently he was caught between a rock and a hard place. But *almost* was the operative word. This man had been willing to kill him and Hannah.

"Tell me who sent you," Luke demanded, hardening his voice.

The man pressed his lips together.

Feeling the touch of Hannah's hand on his arm, Luke gave her a questioning look.

He turned his head so the guy couldn't see his face and mouthed, "You've got an idea?"

She jerked her head to the side, and he followed her a little distance away, where they could talk without being overheard but where he could still keep his eye on the man.

"He's scared," she said.

"No kidding."

"You had the right idea when you offered him transportation out of here."

"He thinks he knows me. He thinks I'm lying when I say I don't know who he works for."

She opened her mouth to answer, when a shot from above rang out. The man on the ground gave a gurgling scream, and a circle of blood soaked the front of his shirt.

Reinforcements had arrived, or the other gunman, the one who had gotten away, was back. And he'd taken out his partner.

Keeping under cover, Luke returned the fire, but the man had already dodged around a corner of the trail and disappeared from sight once more.

"Stay here," he shouted at Hannah as he gave chase.

HANNAH WATCHED Luke take off up the trail, then squatted beside the wounded man, feeling a strange sense of déjà vu.

A few months ago she'd knelt beside a boy watching the life ebb out of him. Then it had been dark and cold. Now the sun was beating down on the man sprawled in front of her with blood spreading rapidly across his shirt.

When she pulled the placket open, she found a mangled mess of flesh. The bullet had missed his heart, because blood was still pumping from the wound, but not his lung, judging from the way he was gasping for breath.

He raised his eyes to her. For a terrible moment, she saw Sean Naylor's face. "Help me."

The Mexican accent snapped her back to the here and now.

"I'll do what I can," she answered, wadding up the bottom of his shirt and pressing it against the wound, pressed hard. But she felt as if she was holding back a flood with a sponge.

"I'm dying," he whispered.

She didn't bother lying to him. "Tell me what you have against Luke."

"Lucas." He was silent for several moments after uttering the name, and she thought he wasn't going to say any more.

"You'll feel easier in your mind if you tell."

His lips moved. "He's a bad *hombre*. He brings the others here. Now the boss…is angry with him…"

"No!" Hannah felt the hairs on the back of her neck stir. This man's dying statement confirmed what Luke had been telling her all along. That he was a criminal.

"Who is angry with him?" she asked urgently.

"The big man…the boss. Bad…" His voice trailed off. He was gone, his sightless eyes staring into the distance.

She was still kneeling beside him when a flash of movement made her scramble for the gun she'd laid in the dust. Then Luke's face and form registered in her bruised brain. He was breathing hard. His shirt was damp with perspiration and his shoulders were sagging.

Standing, she moved away from the dead man, answering Luke's questioning look with a nod.

He looked from her to the body. "I've put you in a position where you got to repeat the worst experience of your life."

A denial leaped to her lips. "No, this was a lot different. He wasn't some scared kid in the wrong place at the wrong time. He and his partner came out here for the purpose of ambushing us. We turned the tables on them. Then his friend finished him off."

He nodded tightly.

She kept her gaze fixed on him as she stood. "Luke, what happened here wasn't all bad. I proved something important to myself." Swallowing, she continued. "I was afraid that the next time I was under fire, I'd freeze up. But I did okay. More than okay. That means more to me than you know."

He crossed to her, clasped her hand, and she knit her fingers with his. After a moment he said, "The bad news is that I didn't catch up with the other guy."

"That's not your fault."

His eyes went to the dead man. "Did he give you any information, say anything I ought to know about?"

Hannah stared at Luke, her mouth gone suddenly dry as the desert sand under her boots. God, now what? Should she lie and say nothing, or tell the truth and confirm Luke's worst fears—that he was a criminal?

CHAPTER THIRTEEN

Once she'd called him the Outlaw. Now Hannah knew deep in her heart it wasn't true. Making a split-second decision, she said, "No. He was too far gone to say anything useful."

By strict interpretation, she wasn't lying, she told herself. All she was doing was making the decision that knowing what the man had said wouldn't be of any help to Luke.

He studied her for several heartbeats, and she held her breath, waiting for another question that she might have to answer with an evasion. Instead, he gave a tight nod. Then the look on his face changed to relief.

She assumed he was responding to her assurance until he said, "Thank God you're all right."

He reached for her, and she came into his arms, holding tight. Closing her eyes, she let his strength envelop her. It was a shock to feel him trembling almost as badly as she.

"I couldn't have gotten to those guys without you. You were magnificent," he said, his hands stroking over her shoulders and down her back, gathering her closer.

She laid her head against his shoulder, then raised it again when he muttered, "I'm sorry."

"For what? You saved our lives."

"For dragging you out here with me."

"You didn't drag me. You hired me."

He laughed. "Is that how you see it?"

"How do you see it?"

"That I don't seem to be able to turn you loose. For the past few days I've been telling myself that I had to keep you close so I could keep an eye on you. That's hardly an adequate explanation of what I've been feeling."

"What have you been feeling?" she asked in a breathy voice.

"Too much."

She longed to hear him elaborate. Instead, he eased away. "We can't stay here. We're standing targets."

Looking up, she blinked into the sunlight, aware of her surroundings for the first time since he'd taken her in his arms.

"Come on." He grabbed her hand and led her toward the truck. But despite his earlier warning, he didn't leave immediately. After they'd climbed into the vehicle, he reached behind the seat and pulled out two bottles of water.

Unscrewing the top on one, she gulped the warm liquid, thinking how wonderful it tasted.

When they'd both emptied a bottle, he jerked his head toward the body they'd left lying on the ground. "As a former police detective, you know we have to report this guy's death to the authorities."

"Yes. But we can't do it now. The last time I tried, my phone wasn't working."

"We could drive straight back into town and notify the sheriff's office."

"Is that what you want to do?"

"No. I want to find out what's farther up this road, because I know that somewhere down that godforsaken track, I'm going to run smack into my past." He stopped, swallowed. "But this time you have a vote."

"I vote for finding out what's farther up the road."

"All right."

"Just like that?"

"We came here to find out who you are."

He looked as if he was about to say something more. Instead, he put the SUV into gear and started off with a lurch.

ADDISON JENNINGS spent every morning reading reports on various Peregrine Connection operations. At any given time, he had men and women working in various parts of the U.S. and in countries as far away as Chile and Albania. They were all on clandestine and sensitive assignments that the U.S. government was funding but would disavow if the secret police of a foreign government or a bloodhound reporter in the United States got wind of a particular operation.

Every man and woman who worked for him knew the risks involved. Every one of them was a patriot willing to take extraordinary chances for the country's national security.

And every one of them had undergone a thorough background investigation—more thorough than if he'd applied for top-secret clearance. Until two days ago, he would have vouched for any of his agents in the Oval Office or to a closed-door congressional committee.

Now he was faced with the painful truth that even a man as experienced as his predecessor could make an error in judgment.

Once again he opened the folder that had been sitting in the middle of his desk blotter. Flipping it open, he stared at the background information, the neatly filled-out forms, the secret reports, the psychological evaluation. The dossier belonged to one of his best operatives. A man who had started out as a raw recruit named Lucas Somerville and had changed aliases many times over the years as circumstances had dictated.

Until last night he'd thought Lucas was dead, killed by a son of a bitch named Vincent Reese.

He'd mourned Lucas. Mourned the loss to the agency. And mourned the loss of the man on a very personal level.

He'd had agents out beating the bushes for Reese ever since, wanting at least the satisfaction of knowing what had happened.

Then he'd gotten the report from a search of the town house in Baltimore. It had been rented in the name of Luke Pritchard.

The man had cleared out in a hurry. Two steps ahead of an assault team. That much was on record. The rest was speculation pieced together from observing what the occupant of the town house had left behind. A man might change his name. He might do a lot to change his appearance. But he didn't change his habits—his methods, the little things that revealed his personality. Like whether he bought four pairs of identical socks or four different colors. Or what foods he stored in his refrigerator.

The Peregrine agents who had searched the house had been pretty sure the man living there was Lucas Somerville.

Lucas Somerville, one of his best men. Gone bad.

Because what other explanation could there be for Somerville's behavior?

He had plenty of money, presumably the money Addison had assumed Reese had stolen. He'd done his utmost to hide his trail—from Dallas Sedgwick's organization and from the Peregrine Connection. Maybe he was even working with Reese, and the two of them had planned this whole thing together.

Addison could only speculate about that. But one thing he did know: Lucas Somerville was on the loose again—one step ahead of Sedgwick's men, and going God knows where and intending to do God knows what.

Addison took a deep breath and let it out in a rush. He'd never ordered that one of his agents be taken dead or alive. Now…

He knew that this one had to be brought to ground. And when Lucas was found, either he had a very good explanation for what he'd been doing or he'd pay the price for his defection.

THE GRAVEL TRACK wound downward among mesquite and scrubby desert oaks.

As they pulled around a stand of river cane, Luke braked. Directly ahead of them was a narrow strip of rounded stones. Beyond the stones, bisecting the road, was the famous river that separated the U.S. from Mexico, the Rio Grande.

It was only about thirty feet wide, as near as Hannah could tell, shallow-looking and full of grayish-beige silt.

They were at an international boundary, where she expected to see a border-patrol outpost, manned by stern-faced troops in their stark green uniforms and their guns in black leather holsters.

But as far as she could tell, there was nobody around besides her and Luke and whatever animals were hiding in the foliage.

"Now what?" she asked.

"We cross."

"Is that legal?"

He shrugged. "Probably not. But it doesn't look like anybody's going to stop us."

Luke got out, and walked to the river. Hannah joined him. They startled a deer who bolted away in the other direction.

She stared after the animal, then turned her attention back to Luke, who stood looking at the water. Reaching for his hand, she knit her fingers with his. It was peaceful here, the quiet pierced only by the occasional call of a bird. Yet the tranquillity was deceptive, she knew. A few miles behind them, men had been waiting in ambush, and she sensed something more ahead.

Still, Luke seemed relaxed as he stared at the flowing water, more at peace with himself than at any other time since she'd met him. To their left was a relatively deep area, where she judged the water might be up to her waist or higher. To the right of the road was a place where the current was faster, flowing rapidly over a stretch of the rounded stones. It looked shallow enough to wade across, certainly shallow enough for the truck to manage.

"Is it always this low?" she asked.

"No. These are drought conditions." He pointed upriver to the rocky stretch. "We'll ford up there."

Hannah followed him back to the SUV, the sound of the door closing behind her echoing in the stillness.

Luke steered the truck to the right, then cautiously entered the water, driving slowly as they forded the river. Hannah held her breath as they crossed the international border, then climbed a low ridge on the other side, where Luke stopped several times, testing the brakes.

They were in Mexico. It looked no different from the Texas landscape they'd just left behind. But it felt different. More dangerous. Certainly to American citizens who were traveling with false identification.

"Do you have any idea where we're going?" she asked.

He pointed to a high plateau that stretched as far as she could see. "Up there."

"You remember that? Specifically?"

He hesitated for a moment. "Not exactly. I don't have any conscious memories. But going up there feels like what I should do."

"And you're going with your feelings?"

He gave her a quick look, then shifted his gaze away. "I guess I've decided it's a waste of time to fight them."

She wanted to ask if he was simply talking about uncovering his past or if he meant more by that comment. But she elected to let the moment pass.

The sun was low in the west as they silently climbed back into the truck.

While the road had been gravel on the U.S. side, here it was fine dirt that sent light-colored dust billowing up on either side of the vehicle.

They reached the edge of the floodplain and the vegetation changed abruptly again as they started climbing along a narrow road that hugged the side of a cliff.

Under any circumstances the drop would have made Hannah nervous. But the narrow road and the lack of a guardrail had her stomach knotting.

They came around a curve, and the whole valley was spread below—too far below as far as she was concerned. When the road angled down again into another valley, she breathed out a little sigh of relief. It ended in a gasp when she felt the tires skid.

Her anxious gaze snapped to Luke as he hit the brake. The truck reduced its speed, but not as much as she would have expected.

"Slow down."

"I'm trying," he answered, his features tight with concentration as he pumped the pedal.

Instead of cooperating, the vehicle was picking up speed.

Luke cursed as they hit a curve going much too fast. All she could do was grab the armrest and hold on tight.

She wanted to close her eyes to block out the rocks rushing past on one side and the drop-off on the other, but she was incapable of looking away as the SUV careened toward the valley below.

Luke reached for the parking brake, slowing them a little, but they were still accelerating dangerously on the narrow, twisting road.

They skidded around another curve, the wheels on the right kicking up stones as they came perilously close to the edge. Thrown to the side, Hannah clenched her teeth, wondering how they were going to make it to the bottom of the hill without flying over the side and sailing into space.

As they came around another curve, she found herself literally staring into blue sky. Jerking the wheel to the right, Luke overcompensated and sideswiped the cliff on the driver's side, sparks flying as metal scraped against stone with a terrible rending noise.

But at least the speed slowed—a little.

Beside her, she could hear the harsh sound of Luke's breathing as he struggled to keep the vehicle under control.

Hannah clung to the seat as they rounded a series of tight curves. Finally they reached the bottom of the long grade, and shot out onto a straightaway.

Jouncing along, Luke hunched forward over the wheel, steering toward the side of the road where sand dragged at the wheels and slowed them down. Foot by foot, she felt the vehicle losing momentum, until they finally came to a halt.

Luke cut the engine and leaned over the wheel, his breath thundering in the sudden silence.

"You are one hell of a driver," she gasped, hardly able to believe they were still in one piece.

"Well, I thought we were gonna go airborne," he admitted in a hoarse voice. Swinging toward her, he held out his arms, and she came into them, clinging with all her strength.

"Are you all right?" he asked, pressing his cheek to hers.

"Yes. What happened?"

He considered the question for a moment. "There are a couple of possibilities. Either the brake line was nicked when they were shooting at us. Or the guy who lent us this SUV was paid to make sure we didn't come back."

She looked around at the utter desolation, remembering what she'd first thought when they turned off the main road. Getting stuck out here could be a death sentence. "Either way we're in trouble," she murmured.

"Yeah."

"What are we going to do?"

"Give me a minute." Luke got out and inspected the side of the truck. Hannah joined him, stepping carefully to avoid descending into the prickly clutches of some purple cactus.

The damage to the vehicle was strictly bodywork. But there was still the problem with the brakes.

"Well, so much for my trip down the road," he muttered as he looked from the truck to the barren landscape and back again.

Walking to the front of the vehicle, he kept going and disappeared through a gap in the rocks ahead. Hannah followed him to a spot where a deep overhang shaded the ground.

"That looks like a pretty safe place to hide the SUV. If I push, can you steer it in there?" he asked.

"Yes."

They returned to the vehicle, and Hannah climbed into the driver's seat. Luke positioned himself at the rear and started to push. Once they were rolling, it appeared he didn't have too much difficulty moving the truck. And the gap between the boulders was wide enough so that she could pull into the space along the wall.

Luke wiped his hands on his jeans as he surveyed the area.

Then, picking up a piece of tumbleweed that had lodged between two rocks, he returned to the road and began brushing away the tire tracks as well as the footprints they'd made.

Hannah found another piece of brush and helped him obliterate the evidence of their passage.

"Are we going to stay here for the night?" she asked, looking up at the sun, which was low in the western sky. Probably they had only an hour or so of daylight left.

He followed the direction of her gaze before bringing his eyes back to her.

"That sounds like our best bet. Sorry, I seem to be treating you to another night of roughing it. At least I don't have to sweep the SUV for black widow spiders. We'll be secure in there."

That took care of tonight. What about tomorrow? She kicked at a small rock and sent it skittering across the ground. "Can we walk out of here? And if we have to, which direction do we go?" she asked.

He looked back down the road. "It's not that bad a hike back to the river. If worst comes to worst, we can follow the shoreline. And eventually we'll make it to civilization." He gave a short laugh. "Maybe we'll even get rescued by the border patrol."

"In that case, I vote for crossing back to the American side as soon as possible."

"Yeah. But right now, we'd better figure out the lay of this land."

She nodded, watching as he walked around the rocks, inspecting the area. When he disappeared from view, she propped her hips against the truck, waiting for him to return.

He'd said some revealing things to her today. Not as much as she wanted to hear but enough to give her hope.

When he reappeared, his voice made her jump.

"This is as safe a location as we could hope for. And there's a spring coming out of the rocks up that way. I wouldn't drink the water, but it's fine for washing. You want to get cleaned up?"

"Yes."

She followed him back the way he'd come, into a narrow canyon, seeing the signs of water immediately in the relative lushness of the vegetation. The ground was damp underfoot, and he led her up a path covered with tracks—deer and other animals'—to a spot where water tumbled from a crevice in the rock into a small, clear pool bordered by grass and some purple flowers. It was a beautiful setting, one that they never would have discovered under ordinary circumstances.

And there was more.

"Look." Luke pointed to the wall on the other side of the pool.

Hannah followed his gaze and found herself staring at a series of drawings on the rock. The bodies depicted there were almost rectangular, and the rendering stylized. Yet she saw the unmistakable outline of human forms, with arms outstretched and some kind of plumes rising from their heads.

"What are those?"

"Shamans. The drawings have religious significance. Or magical. Take your pick. Nobody knows for sure because the people who drew them disappeared thousands of years ago."

"How do you know?"

He shrugged. "I just do." His expression turned suddenly angry. "All the general knowledge is there. Tons of useful skills and useless facts. It's just the personal stuff that's vanished. It's like in that book by Stephen King. *The Dead Zone.* About a guy who was in a coma and woke up with chunks missing from his memory. It turned out he had a brain tumor."

"You don't have a brain tumor."

"I have some pretty weird gaps in my gray matter. It's like selective amnesia. If it has anything personal to do with Lucas Somerville, it's AWOL."

"It'll come back. You just need the right trigger."

"You mean like meeting the woman who raised me after my mother ran away? Or like spending the night in the house where I grew up? You'd think if anything was gonna do the trick, one of those experiences would have."

"Obviously your childhood was painful. I don't blame you for blocking it out."

"Painful, yeah. Like whatever happened out here in the desert. I don't want to remember that either. I must hate myself so much that I don't want anything to do with Lucas Somerville!"

The words and the tone of his voice pierced her. Somehow, in this quiet canyon, he'd managed to say what he'd bottled up inside himself for so long.

She ached to reach for him. But she saw a closed look shutter his face and knew he was regretting his outburst.

The emotions were too raw to share with anyone, especially her.

Probably if he'd felt free to do so, he would have left her standing there. But not when they were stranded in the middle of the desert.

So she helped him out by turning away and walking toward the pool. Cupping her hands under the small waterfall, she washed the dust off her face and neck. Her motions were smooth and mechanical, but her mind was churning with a sudden compulsion. Raising her eyes, she looked at the ancient drawings painted on the canyon wall.

Luke had said they were magical.

Ancient magic.

Thousands of years ago people had believed that this was a place of power. And now she felt the potency enfolding her.

Back in Baltimore she would have felt foolish calling on ancient, primitive forces. Now she mouthed a plea under her breath. "Help him," she begged. "If you have any power left, help him unlock the secrets he's hidden from himself."

After she'd said it, she did feel foolish. Was she really asking help from medicine men who had lived thousands of years ago?

Stepping away from the water, she said in a neutral voice, "Your turn."

He walked to the water, pulled his gun from the waistband of his jeans and set it on a rock. Then he washed the dust from his hands before wetting his face and neck the way she'd done.

"Probably it would feel good on your back and shoulders, too," she advised.

"Yeah." He stripped off his shirt, tossed it onto a rock and leaned into the flow of water, angling so that it sluiced over his broad back.

He looked primitive and magnificent, she thought as she watched the play of muscles across his shoulders. He stayed with his back to her for a long time, the rays of reddening sunlight burnishing his skin.

He was such a strong man, even if he didn't realize it. Terrible things had happened to him, things that would have crushed a lesser individual. Even when his brain had locked away memories that he needed, he had forced himself to work around the excruciating disability. Lord, he must feel as if he was trapped inside a surreal painting—and there's no way to claw his way back to the outside world.

And worse than that, he was afraid he was a criminal. Even when she knew to the depths of her soul that it couldn't be true.

She clenched and unclenched her hands at her sides as she thought how alone he must feel. And how determined he was not to drag her in there with him.

"Luke?"

"Um?"

"You're not going to tell me you have to stand guard duty tonight," she said in a voice that sounded far more steady than she felt.

"What was true last night is still true."

She shook her head, focusing on an assessment of the danger. "Last night we were at a specific house at a specific ranch. Tonight we could be anywhere along a hundred-mile stretch of road. Well, not on the road, actually. We're hidden from view."

His features hardened. "All that's true, but if you know what's good for you, you'll stay as far away from me as you can get."

The look in his eyes might have frightened her if she hadn't come to understand him so well since those first nights when they'd checked each other out in the Last Chance Bar.

Then she'd known he was attracted to her. Now she knew that he needed her more than anyone had ever needed her in her life, even if he kept putting barriers between them. His mistrust of her. His mistrust of himself. They were all rolled up in the same package.

"I'm not running away from you," Hannah whispered. "And I'm not letting you run away, either. Not from me."

Pretending she wasn't shaking inside, she took a step forward and reached for him.

CHAPTER FOURTEEN

Her breath caught and held in her throat as she waited to see what he would do. When his arms came up to enfold her, some of the terrible uncertainty eased out of her.

For a long moment they simply stood clinging to each other as the light faded around them. From somewhere above came the sound of a bird calling, but it was far away. The whole world was far away. There was only her and Luke in this private place where the power of ancient spells gathered about them.

The power awed her, energized her.

"Do you think the shamans did magic rituals here?" she whispered.

"Yes," he answered with absolute conviction.

"You and I have our own magic."

He stared down at her. "What do you mean?"

"Against all odds, we found each other. And we found this place. It would be a shame to waste it on anything trivial."

She didn't know if he took her meaning. She was telling him that if the two of them made love, the act would carry power far beyond the mere physical union of two people. She felt it in the depths of her soul. Perhaps he felt some of the magic, too, because they moved at the same instant. She reached up, and he lowered his head so that their mouths met and held in a kiss that was sweeter than they had exchanged before.

Sweet, yet building to a steady, insistent passion that swamped her senses. Dizzy with it, she tried to show him how she felt with her lips, her tongue, her teeth, her hands sliding possessively over the naked skin of his back and shoulders.

They clung together, swaying on their feet as though they were both too giddy to stand without holding on to each other.

He took a step back, propping his hips against the wall, splaying his legs to equalize their heights, then gathering her to him.

As she moved against the rigid flesh behind the fly of his jeans, white-hot sensation shot through her body.

He had taken control now, kissing her with a driving need that fueled her passion. When his fingers found the hem of her shirt and pulled it upward, she angled her torso back so that he could pull the shirt over her head and toss it away. Then he worked the catch at the back of her bra, sending that garment after the shirt.

When he took the weight of her breasts in his hands, she drew in a quick, gasping breath. Then his fingers crested over the tips, and the breath turned into a sob.

She wanted to tell him how good it felt. But it was impossible to say more than his name.

"Luke."

"Darlin' Hannah."

He touched her, kissed her, worked the snap of her jeans and then the zipper so that he could stroke the heart of her and she felt his touch with the force of a storm roaring through her.

"Lucas, I need you," she breathed, knowing now that the need was something she had never experienced before. It was so different from what she had felt with Gary. Then she'd been running away from emotions she couldn't handle. Now she was running headlong toward something precious—joining with the only man who could make her whole. And only she could do the same for him.

"Yes," he growled, though she suspected he still didn't fully understand what making love with her would mean. But he would.

He was starting to pull her down to the sandy ground when he stopped abruptly, raised his head and cursed.

As his hands left her heated body, her eyes blinked open, and a kind of terrible panic seized her.

"Luke, please. Don't stop. Not this time."

"I— We can't do this here. Not here."

She had been lost to everything but the deep sense of connection with this man. Now the time and the place filtered into her consciousness: the desert, with night fast approaching. Not a good combination.

"Come on. We have to get back to the SUV before we get lost in the dark."

A shiver traveled over her skin as the words sank in. Looking around, she searched for the clothing they'd discarded. There was still enough light to spot her white T-shirt and bra. Hastily she pulled on the shirt and stuffed the bra into her pocket.

Luke didn't bother with his shirt. Grabbing his gun, he led her rapidly back the way they'd come. Hannah hurried to keep up. The magical little canyon had overwhelmed her and now her heart was thumping. She moved to Luke's side, glad of his strong arm around her as they retraced their steps, her eyes scanning the ground and the rocks above them for anything that slithered or rattled or hissed.

Some of the tension dissipated as they reached the mouth of the canyon. But before they'd taken half a dozen steps, she saw a gray, menacing shape gliding through the darkness, then another and another. Animal shapes—the size of large dogs, with bristled fur and long snouts.

She stopped still in her tracks, and the gray shapes did the same.

The thought flashed in her mind that she'd been wrong all along. These were demons materializing out of the desert to claim the canyon for their own.

Even as the idea formed she knew it was nonsense. Her brain told her she was looking at a small herd of incredibly ugly flesh-and-blood creatures. But reason did nothing to stop the scream that tore from her throat as she reached for her gun. When they heard the sound, the beasts turned and ran. At the same time, Luke grabbed her hand, stopping her from shooting.

"Don't!"

"But—"

"Those are javelinas. Wild pigs. They live in the desert. They were coming to the canyon for water."

She leaned weakly against Luke, her pulse pounding, trying to collect her scattered wits.

"Pigs? In the desert?"

"Yeah. The only native pigs in North America. This is their territory. I'm sure we scared the spit out of them showing up unannounced at their watering hole." He wrapped her hand in his and moved forward. "Come on. We'd better get back to the SUV."

He started off again, and she followed him across the sandy ground, hoping he knew where they'd left the vehicle, because she had no idea.

She was about to ask him if he was sure of the direction when the dark shape of the truck loomed in front of them, moonlight glinting off the painted surface.

"Stay here," Luke commanded, speaking under his breath.

She stopped, waiting as he left her side and moved cautiously toward the vehicle, his gun drawn.

Pulling open the back door, he stood for a moment with the gun covering the interior, then turned back to her.

"All clear. Come on."

She looked up at the glorious canopy of stars sparkling in the black velvet of the sky and felt caught once more by the magic of this place. A line from an old Eagles song drifted through her mind—a line about making love in the desert with the radiance of the stars shining down.

Were they going to make love?

Or had Luke come to his senses? At least she thought that was the way he'd put it, even if he was wrong, so very wrong.

Straightening, she joined him. When she reached his side, she said, "Fold the seat down."

He stood regarding her in the moonlight. "Somebody could have heard you scream."

She kept her voice even. "Are you using that as an excuse to back away from me?"

"I should."

She managed a shaky laugh. "What's your alternative? Spending the night outside with the snakes and the pigs?"

Without answering, he slipped behind the wheel and turned on the engine long enough to roll down the front windows several inches. Then he folded down the backrest, making a wide, flat surface.

Hannah climbed inside, propping her back against the front seat and stretching out her legs as she waited to see whether Luke was going to join her—or climb into the front seat instead. When he slipped into the cargo area and closed the door behind him, she felt some of her tension ease.

The moon and the stars gave her enough light to see the stark lines of his profile. Reaching out a hand, she stroked his cheek, turned his face toward her.

"Hannah…you don't know what you're getting into with me," he said in a gritty voice.

She had conquered her own doubts in the magic canyon, and gone far beyond those doubts. But she understood the uncertainty that tore at him.

"I know as much as I need to. Stop beating yourself up because you can't remember your past. I know you're waiting for it to come back and bite you. But if you had half as much faith in yourself as I have in you, you'd give the two of us a chance right now."

She saw naked need in his eyes but knew he wouldn't be the one to ask for what he craved most.

Smiling, her eyes never leaving him, she pulled her shirt over her head and tossed it into the front seat. Then she pulled off her boots and worked the snap at her waistband, discarding her jeans and her panties at the same time.

"Hannah." The way he said her name made her heart stop, then start again in a fast, erratic rhythm.

Gathering her to himself, he kissed her. It wasn't a tender kiss. It was hot and wild, transporting them both back to where they'd left off in the canyon.

LUKE BROKE AWAY long enough to kick off his own jeans and boots, then swept her naked body against his, holding her as he devoured her mouth, then slid lower to kiss her neck and shoulders.

Had he ever needed a woman as much as he needed Hannah? If he had, he couldn't imagine it. All he knew was that he had felt a deep connection to her from the moment he had seen her.

And now there was no denying the passion roaring through him.

When he dipped his head and drew one of her pebble-hard nipples into his mouth, she moaned her pleasure, the sound pouring into him.

He forgot where they were and how they had gotten there. Forgot any sense of caution. Forgot everything but the piercing ecstasy of being with her. Finally.

When his fingers stroked down her body and delved into hot, slick feminine flesh, she sobbed as she arched into the caress.

He might be a man without conscious memories. But he discovered one good thing about himself that night. He knew how to please a woman. And he silently thanked God for that skill as he pushed her higher and higher still until she was quivering in his arms, her fingers digging into his shoulders.

"Luke, please. Now."

It was a plea he was helpless to deny. His body covered hers, claimed hers, stunning him with a kind of intensity beyond his imagining.

He made a hoarse sound deep in his chest, unable to express in words what he was feeling. How much he was feeling.

Thankful for the moonlight and the canopy of stars above them, he stared into her face. She gazed up at him, reached to gently touch her fingertips to his cheek, his lips.

"Finally," she whispered.

For heartbeats, he was still, poised above her, the two of them joined but quiescent. Then the longing to move his hips became more than he could bear. As he thrust into her, their mutual need flared.

Sexual need. Emotional need. And something more that he

couldn't name, but could only experience with an intensity that made him tremble.

Heat surged through his body. Not just the heat of erotic contact but heat that burned through his brain, seared his flesh to the bone.

He was aware of intense pleasure and of more—of his mind wavering on the brink of discovery, his mind finally free and soaring, like a great bird riding an invisible current of wind far above the earth.

He had stopped thinking.

There was only physical pleasure. And at the same time a kind of peace that transcended his conscious memory.

He quickened the rhythm, taking Hannah with him to a high desert plateau where the air was almost too thin to breathe. She clung to him, her body trembling as she approached the summit. And when he felt the inner contractions take her, he let his own control slip.

She called his name. His real name. "Lucas. Lucas." And for the first time it meant something to him, as though she were calling him through a doorway into another existence.

His own climax shook him, a giant earthquake rolling through his body and soul, through his brain. A shock wave so deep and profound that it left him weak and trembling as he collapsed on top of her.

For a confused moment he thought he was back in the canyon by the pool of water, staring up at the mystical drawings on the wall. The ancient artist spoke to him in a language that he couldn't understand, telling him things that he already knew.

He knew! Because once again he was whole. His body and mind connected.

Hannah's hand stroked over his shoulders, winnowed through his hair. "Luke?" she murmured.

Her voice brought him back to reality—the reality of his weight pressing down on her. By a massive effort he heaved himself to the side and lay there panting, his head spinning with images and emotions that left him shaking.

He tried to say something—to tell her what had happened to him—but his throat wouldn't work.

She shifted toward him, rising over his chest. "Are you all right?"

He heard panic rising in her voice, knew he had to reassure her. "Yes," he said, although he could still barely speak. He clasped her to him, his arms infused with a strength that had eluded him until now. "I remember." He managed to get out those two words.

She stared down at him with a mixture of wonder and disbelief that mirrored the shock and gratitude he was feeling. "You mean you remember your past?" she asked in a shaky voice.

"Yes." The confirmation sighed out of him. Then he said it more strongly as he felt the precious knowledge expand inside his chest. "Yes."

Hannah found his hand and clasped her fingers with his, holding tight. "Thank God. But how?"

His own fingers clenched so tightly that he was afraid he might hurt her. With a sound low in his throat, he made a deliberate effort to ease up on his grip. How did you explain a miracle? *Could* you explain?

He forced himself to try because he needed to make sense out of what had happened. "I've been pushing myself, trying to find some way to get at the memories locked in my brain. Then we were making love, and I wasn't thinking about anything. I was only feeling the pleasure of it, feeling energy building between us."

She cuddled against him, flattened her hand against his chest, feeling the still-accelerated beat of his heart. "Yes."

"Then...then my mind went soaring free and when it was over, I was suddenly me again. Lucas Somerville. From Pritchard, Texas."

She tipped her face toward him as if she was trying to wrap her mind around the concept.

"It was being with you. I couldn't have done it without you." Leaning forward, he captured her mouth in a long, deep kiss.

Afterward neither one of them spoke for long moments, each still trying to absorb the new reality. Then he felt Hannah shift in his arms.

"Are the memories good or bad?" she asked in a small voice.

He gave a hoarse laugh. "Do you mean am I one of the good guys or the bad guys? The answer is I'm not a dry-gulcher."

"If you're trying to tell me you're not a criminal, I knew that all along."

His next words strove to set the record straight. "Yeah, well, that doesn't mean I'm not in a hell of a lot of trouble."

She leaned forward again, brushed her lips lightly against his. "Whatever it is, we'll face it together."

He played with the ends of her hair as he thought about what he could tell her. Over the years, there were rules he'd never broken. Rules he still shouldn't break. But he'd dragged her into danger, and he thought he owed her an explanation that made sense.

"I work for a government agency," he finally said. "An agency that you've never head of."

"Try me."

"The Peregrine Connection."

"You're right. And that's a pretty strange name."

"The guy who started it was kind of eccentric. During the Cold War, he saw the need for an organization that could slash through red tape like a machete. An organization that could take on jobs that the U.S. government couldn't acknowledge. So he started the Peregrine Connection with his own funds, then found congressional support among senators and congressmen who shared his vision. Our budget is hidden in various appropriations. All our ops are black. And if we run into trouble, we're on our own."

"Like you are now."

"Yeah," he answered, wondering how bad it really was.

"Do you know who raided the town house in Baltimore?" she asked.

"Probably the crime boss who lost the money. Dallas Sedgwick."

"The boss…" she breathed.

The way she said it made him shift toward her, his eyes questioning, the old doubts surfacing even as he tried to hold them back. "What do you know about it?"

She gulped. "The man from the adobe… When he was dying, he said you were bad, that you worked for a boss, that the man was angry with you—" She stopped short, apparently realizing what she'd given away.

He gripped her shoulders. "He told you I was a criminal and you told *me* he hadn't said anything important? Didn't we set some ground rules when I first hired you? You promised to turn me in to the authorities if you found out I was on the wrong side of the law."

He saw her hands twist together. "I knew it wasn't true! And I knew it would only upset you."

He stared at her, trying to absorb the implications. She'd

lied to him, apparently with the best of intentions—to spare him an accusation that would have shattered him.

She lifted her chin. "We know you're not a criminal. So let's get back to what really happened to you," she suggested.

He sighed, knowing she was right, even if he couldn't follow her precise reasoning. He needed to give her the facts, to put her in the picture. "I've spent the past two years establishing an underworld identity for the purpose of getting hired by Sedgwick. His money comes from various sources, a big part of which is smuggling people and drugs across the border between Mexico and the U.S. I'd been with him for six months and I was out here on a big drug deal. Only, somebody knew what was going down and crashed the party."

He sat up and looked off in the direction of the mountains. "I think I know where we're going to find a bunch of dead bodies in the desert. I say *think* because the meeting in the desert is where my memory still fades."

"But you know there *was* a meeting?"

"I set it up."

"I've read that sometimes if you're in an accident and it causes a memory loss, the recollection of the accident and the time just before it may never come back."

"Yeah, I read that, too. I read every damn thing I could find on amnesia—for all the good it did me."

"Where does the memory cut off?"

His mind turned inward as he tried to dredge up every scrap of information he could about the event that had damn near driven him over the edge with frustration and self-doubt. "I remember getting to the meeting location. I remember waiting for the contacts to arrive. But I don't have a clue about what happened after that. I don't know why I've got the money, and how I got away. That part's totally blank."

She pushed herself up beside him, suddenly self-conscious that they were sitting naked in the backseat of an SUV having this conversation.

After their first night roughing it, Luke had bought a blanket. Reaching for the boxes of supplies, she found the blanket and flipped it open, laying it across her lower body and his.

He turned toward her. "Cold?"

"Uh-huh."

Slipping his arm around her, he pulled her closer.

Nestling against him, she returned to the previous topic. "But you remember the Peregrine Connection. You remember the Sedgwick assignment." She stopped and swallowed. "And you remember your childhood."

He grimaced. "Yeah. I can understand why I wanted to blank that last part out."

"Oh, Luke…Lucas. Was it so terrible?"

"My mother…" he started, then stopped.

"Left you—with a man who took out her defection on you."

He closed his eyes then opened them again. "Juanita made it bearable. If… When I get back to Pritchard, I need to tell her that."

SHE WATCHED HIS FACE, knew that he thought he was speaking the truth. But she understood that it hadn't really been bearable. Not for a child with the sensitivities of Lucas Somerville. He had felt unloved. Unwanted. Betrayed. Not just by his mother, but by his father as well, although Hannah was sure he wasn't going to admit that to her. So instead of pressing him, she said, "You will get back."

"Yeah, well, I'm not going to sugarcoat the situation.

We're in danger from Sedgwick's men. And in danger from whoever it was that double-crossed Sedgwick. Or whatever happened out here. So it would be a hell of a lot more convenient if we had a working vehicle so we could hightail it back to civilization."

"So what are we going to do?" she asked, giving herself points for keeping her voice steady.

"Tomorrow we're going to the rendezvous point and see if we can figure out what happened. Then we're hiking back to the river and following it to the nearest phone so I can contact my real boss, Addison Jennings."

"Good. Because it will be a long time before I want to visit the desert again."

"Your baptism of fire."

She leaned her head on his shoulder, unwilling to voice her thoughts. She should be worried. She should be frightened. But all she could think about was Luke.

She loved him, but she had no idea if he could accept that. Not when the first woman he'd loved—his mother—had walked away from him.

So she kept silent. For now she'd have to be content with knowing she was a good judge of character, that she hadn't given her heart to one of the bad guys.

And after they got out of this mess? Well, she suspected she still wasn't in for an easy time. He hadn't said much about the secret agency where he worked—the Peregrine Connection—or his assignments. But she could read between the lines of his brief description. As one of their operatives, he'd been living on the edge—without family ties, without attachments. He'd chosen that life.

She felt her heart squeeze. Maybe he'd chosen to be an outsider because, coming from his background, that was the only life he was capable of leading. Even when he hadn't remembered his identity, he'd been finding reasons for not getting close to her. His amnesia. His doubts about her loyalty.

Now he knew who he was, and he could come up with a whole host of other reasons for keeping his distance. The speculation sent a little tremor through her, and she knew she'd feel a whole lot better if she could hear some kind of commitment from him. Instead, she turned so that her breasts were pressed against his chest, pleased by the reaction it was impossible for him to hide. He wanted her, and that was a good start.

He gave her a quick kiss on the cheek. "I'm telling you we're in danger—and you want to fool around?"

She dropped her gaze to where the blanket covered his lap. "It appears you do, too."

He stroked his finger down her naked arm. "Water first. And food."

"Water and food," she repeated. "I forgot about them."

He reached for one of the boxes of supplies, pulled out a water bottle and handed it to her.

She twisted off the cap and took a long swallow, then opened one of the packages of peanut butter crackers.

When she saw him watching her, she smiled. "What are you thinking about?"

"How different this is from last night."

"I like it a lot better." She scooted closer so that her shoulder was against his, watching him bite into a cracker and thinking that this was the most erotic meal she had ever shared.

THE PHONE RANG on the bedside table, and Addison Jennings's eyes snapped open. Four in the morning. It must be important.

"Jennings," he said as he reached for the phone.

"This is Jed Prentiss."

The name meant nothing to him.

"You don't know me," the voice on the other end of the line confirmed. "But I used to work for the Falcon," the man continued, using Amherst Gordon's old code name. "In the late eighties, early nineties."

"Go on," Addison said, pressing the button that would record the conversation and slipping out of bed to the desk where a workstation was connected to the main Peregrine computer. Quickly his hands moved over the keyboard, finding the right file.

A Jed Prentiss had worked for Gordon. And the dates matched. Yet there was no guarantee this man was Prentiss.

"I know you're checking your files," the caller said. "You'll see I ran into some problems on a Caribbean Island called Royale Verde." He cleared his throat. "The disability I acquired eventually led to my resignation."

"And…"

"I have some important information about one of your agents. Lucas Somerville."

Addison's senses sharpened. "Go on," he said in a neutral voice.

"The reason he hasn't contacted you is that he has amnesia."

Addison felt the hairs on the back of his neck stir. "And how would you know that?"

"I work for Randolph Security. We have an association with a detective agency in Baltimore. He hired a P.I. to help him discover his identity. You probably know about the raid on his town house. Either it was carried out by you or by the crime boss looking for his missing million dollars."

"What guarantee do I have that you're telling the truth? Or that you're even who you say you are?"

"You've got a voiceprint of mine on record. Compare it to your recording of this message. The point is, I know your man is trying to figure out who he is. And I know the way *your* mind works, if you're following Amherst Gordon's pattern. You probably think he's defected. I'm telling you that he'd have reported in if he knew who he was. And I'm asking you not to go after him."

"Why are you going out on a limb for him?"

"Because he's with my P.I. friend, Hannah Dawson. And if anything happens to her because of you, I'd consider it an act of extreme hostility, if you take my meaning."

The line went dead.

Addison was in the process of sending a message to the Peregrine operations room when the phone rang again.

This time it was Senator Martinson, the man who had been instrumental in keeping the flow of money coming to the Peregrine Connection. Martinson was a hard-nosed son of a bitch. But he'd been useful. Lately he'd been throwing his weight around.

"Senator," Addison said. "What can I do for you so early in the morning?"

Martinson got right to the point. "I understand an initiative in Texas blew up in your face several weeks ago."

Addison's hand clenched on the phone. "Where did you get that information?"

"It's my business to keep abreast of your operations."

From whom? Was there someone on the Peregrine staff leaking information to the senator? In the old days, the idea would have been unthinkable. Now it looked like a distinct possibility.

"I've backed you to the hilt. I expect you to return the favor. I'm coming up for reelection, and I want to make sure that this doesn't turn into an embarrassment for my committee. If your little flap down in Texas makes the *Washington Post,* I'm in deep trouble."

"We're doing our best, Senator."

"One of your operatives went bad. Deal with him."

"I've just received information that there may be extenuating circumstances."

"Deal with him. And his woman accomplice. If this comes out smelling like manure, I'm the one who will have to call the hearings to investigate. And you don't want your dirty linen washed in public."

The threat seemed to thicken the air around Addison, making it difficult to breathe.

They talked for several more minutes, Addison clenching the receiver more tightly as the conversation went on.

When he hung up, he was feeling sick, physically and emotionally. The Peregrine Connection had been set up to take on assignments that other agencies didn't dare touch. And they'd operated under the cloak of secrecy. If they didn't have that, they were as exposed and vulnerable as a beetle lying on its back with its underbelly in the air.

He'd have to take the steps necessary to change the situation, because the agency was too valuable an asset to lose. But corrections would take time. For the short run, if it came down to weighing the life of one man against the good of the organization, there was only one way to call the play.

THE BRUSH OF LUCAS'S LIPS against her cheek woke Hannah just before dawn.

She smiled and reached for him, but he pulled away from her, looking down into her face with a regretful expression.

"I'm sorry I've got to wake you up, but we've got a

pretty good walk ahead of us. I'd like to get started while it's cool."

Pushing herself up, she rubbed her eyes.

"I thought about it. If I could stash you here, I would. But I can't leave you in the middle of the desert."

"I wouldn't let you do that anyway."

"Yeah, I figured."

They dressed, drank more water and strapped on the small backpacks that he'd included with their supplies, then ate some trail mix as they walked.

A half hour later, Hannah knew why Luke had started early. The sun was brutal above them, the heat already like an oven.

By the time they reached the mountains, her shirt was plastered to her body and sweat was trickling freely down her body.

Luke looked at her appraisingly, then ordered her to take a drink. She didn't need a second invitation. But she rationed the water, figuring that she might need it more later.

Reaching the mountains was a relief. At least there was some shade as they wound their way up a steep trail carved through stark rocks.

Twice more they stopped for water, although Hannah suspected Luke was also using the opportunity to let her catch her breath. She had kept up her exercise schedule when she'd left the police force, and she'd thought she was in good shape. But that was in Baltimore. In the desert, the relentless heat was taking its toll on her stamina.

When they came to a place where the trail forked, he stopped again, and she leaned against a rock, trying not to look as if she was winded.

She could see Luke was wound tight as a mainspring as he chose the trail to the right and started moving again.

She didn't waste her breath asking if they were getting close to their destination. Instead, she simply kept plodding along in back of him, determined to keep up the pace. He came around a curve, stopped short and stepped back, blocking the middle of the path.

The stench coming from the other side of the rock told her what he was blocking from view.

Something very dead. She shouldered past Luke—then gagged. There were six bodies, and all of them had been in the hot sun for much too long.

"Sedgwick's men?" she asked.

"Yeah. And another guy. Someone I don't recognize."

They both stepped back around the rock where they didn't have to confront the carnage. She'd seen bodies before, but not bodies like these.

"You think you can figure out what happened?" she asked in a choked voice.

Before he could answer, another voice chimed in. "I'd like to hear the answer to that, too."

The speaker was a man with an automatic pistol in his hand.

"Take out your guns, nice and easy," he said. "And drop them on the ground. Then raise your hands."

CHAPTER FIFTEEN

Hannah stood facing the man with the gun, struggling to project an aura of calm even when her heart was pounding so hard inside her chest that she felt as if she was going to faint.

Without making any sudden moves, she pulled the gun from the waistband of her jeans and tossed it on the ground, then raised her hands.

Beside her, Luke silently did the same, his eyes never wavering from the man who had surprised them.

Who was this guy? One of Sedgwick's men? Had he stationed someone out here round the clock in the middle of nowhere? Or was this someone from the Mexican authorities?

"Let the woman go. She had nothing to do with what happened here," Luke said.

"We'll see. Show me where you stashed the money."

"Not around here."

"You expect me to believe that? Then why did you come back—to make sure your friends are still dead?"

"I have my reasons."

"You're going to turn the cash over to me," he said, his voice flat and his eyes as cold as a lizard's.

"I don't think so."

"If you don't talk, the lady is going to get hurt," the gunman answered.

Hannah studied him with a strange sense of detachment, as if she were on the other side of a one-way mirror looking at an individual in an interrogation room. The way he spoke, his malevolent expression, told her that he had no conscience. He intended to leave her and Luke as dead as the men they'd just encountered.

Luke was speaking again. "The money's in a safe place, but if you want to get your hands on it, you'll need my cooperation."

"I don't need you. The lady will tell me."

"She doesn't know."

The gunman considered for a moment. "Then this is how we'll play it—you'll tell me, to keep her from getting shot in the kneecap and left out here for the buzzards."

She saw Luke's complexion go gray and knew their captor hadn't missed the reaction.

"All right. The money's buried about twenty miles from here."

Hannah processed the information. Luke had just told a bald-faced lie.

"Nice try. What are you trying to do—buy yourself some time?"

"No," Luke answered, his voice unwavering.

"Where exactly? Hurry up or your girlfriend gets it now."

She saw Luke's jaw harden, saw a look of bone-chilling anger come into his eyes. "The money's in a little canyon with a natural spring," he said, describing the place where they'd been the night before. "I put it in a nice safe hidey-hole where nobody's gonna stumble over it. And if you touch a hair on her head, I won't tell you a damn thing."

The man with the gun contemplated him for agonizing heartbeats. Finally he said, "Then I guess you're damn well going to have to show me. But if I find out you're lying, she gets it first. Then you."

Luke said nothing, only nodded.

"Okay, I'm parked on the other side."

Hannah had no idea what he meant. The other side of what? He confused her even more as he gestured toward what looked like a solid wall of rock behind him.

Stepping aside, the man narrowed his eyes and pointed the gun at Luke. "You first. Through the cave. And don't try anything funny, like getting too far ahead of me. You make a wrong move and your lady suffers the consequences."

Hannah clenched her teeth to keep her jaw steady. If they got to that canyon and Luke couldn't produce the money, they were in big trouble. So somewhere between here and the canyon, he had to be planning on their getting away. But how? And where?

As he passed her, he said something under his breath. It sounded like "Nasty critters."

Just the two low words as their eyes met for a brief, fierce instant.

The man with the gun had heard him, too. "What was that? What the hell did you say?" he demanded.

Luke raised his chin. "Just an editorial comment."

"About what?"

"You."

"Get going before I shoot you here."

Luke strode down the narrow gap. As Hannah watched his tight shoulders, she puzzled over what he'd said.

Nasty critters. The phrase was important enough for him to risk a comment now, of all times. He'd said critters. Not critter. He wasn't talking about the man who held them captive. He was trying to tell her something. But what?

She turned the phrase over in her mind as Luke led the way toward the rock wall. When she followed, she spotted what she hadn't seen from several yards away. The path turned a sharp corner into a covered passage.

The cave had a high roof and an uneven floor that slanted downward toward another opening—so that light filtered in from two directions.

Luke stopped abruptly at the entrance to the tunnel.

"Get going!" the man with the gun snapped.

"Give me a minute for my eyes to adjust. You know damn well it's dangerous in here. One wrong move and you could go over the edge. Or step on some nasty critters."

Hannah took in the words. *Nasty critters.* He'd said it again.

Behind her, she could hear their captor shifting impatiently from foot to foot. Then Luke started forward. Dry-mouthed, she followed, aware every second that a gun was pointed at her back.

The light was dim, and the temperature was several degrees cooler than outside, cooling the perspiration on her neck.

Luke was certainly right about the place being dangerous. There was a rock wall on the left, then a narrow walkway a couple of feet wide strewn with fallen rubble. To make matters worse, part of the surface had crumbled away, where the ledge dropped suddenly off into darkness.

Luke turned and pointed toward a pile of loose rocks. "Watch your step. You could slip if you're not real careful."

"I'll catch her if she does!" the gunman replied, then switched on a flashlight.

Shuddering at the prospect of his dirty hands touching her flesh, Hannah pressed a palm against the rough rock wall to steady herself physically and mentally, too.

Trying to get her bearings, she looked around and was astonished to see paintings like the ones in the little canyon with the watering hole.

Going stark still, she stared at the stylized figures. The shamans had been here, she thought in wonder, her eyes taking in the sweep of images that marched along the rock wall a few feet above her head.

"Get moving!" the man in back of her ordered.

"I'm scared of the dark," she managed to say, making her voice quiver.

He made a derisive sound, then raised the light so that it played along the ledge by her feet. "I'll give you something to be scared of if you don't move."

Automatically, she took a step forward. But her mind was spinning now. This was a magic place like the canyon last night where Luke had taken her in his arms. She'd felt it then. And she felt it now in a rush of cool sensation that helped to center her.

Still, her pulse was pounding as she crept forward, feeling as if the world had slowed around her, giving her the time she needed. Time to remember something important.

"I said hurry up," the man behind her growled. "We haven't got all day."

"I'm going as fast as I can," she answered, hearing her own voice come from far away. Her eyes were riveted to the wall beside her, all her senses alert for something that should be obvious. The drawings? Was there something in the drawings that would help her?

Several feet in front of her, she spotted a place where the artist had painted a cluster of black dots like a clump of spiders clinging to the vertical surface. As she focused on them, Luke's words leaped into her head. *Nasty critters.*

Luke had said *nasty critters*. Twice. Telling her there could be dangers in this cool, dark place. Dangers real or imagined, she suddenly realized.

It was then that she understood what he wanted her to do. Throw the man behind her off balance.

Carefully she picked her moment, waiting until she had just passed a pile of loose rubble that had shifted dangerously under her feet, sending a spray of chips over the edge of the narrow ledge. Then she drew in a breath. Stopping in her tracks, she let out a scream of terror that echoed and re-echoed off the stone walls of the tunnel.

"Black widow spiders!" she shrieked like a helpless female in a horror movie, her voice rising in feigned panic as she ducked down and covered her head with her hands.

"Where?" the gunman shouted from behind her.

"Over there!" Frantically she pointed, cowering back.

He was almost on top of her now. So close that his pant legs brushed against her boots.

From her crouched position, she pushed backward, catching him in the knees, tipping him off balance on the narrow stone walkway.

As he scrabbled to get his feet back under him, he dropped the flashlight and squeezed the trigger of the gun, sending bullets glancing wildly off the rock. Then the gun, too, clanked to the ledge and went over the side.

"Stay down," Luke shouted.

She grabbed for the weapon, missed it, then flattened herself against the rock as Luke leaped over her, head lowered as he butted their captor in the stomach.

She heard a scream as the man tried to right himself. Turning, she saw him grab desperately for purchase, clawing at the rock wall, even as he pitched over the edge of the walkway and tumbled into space, his scream of horror echoing off the cave walls as he fell through the darkness.

Long moments later, she heard him hit the bottom somewhere far below, but the flashlight had gone out when it tumbled over, so she could see nothing. The gun was down there, too.

Stunned, she could only stare into the blackness. It had all happened so fast that she could hardly believe it was over until Luke grabbed her. Pulling her into his arms, he wrapped her in a grip so tight that it was almost impossible for her to breathe.

EYES CLOSED, Luke clung to her with equal strength, feeling the pounding of her heart and his.

When he thought about what had almost happened, he felt cold, clammy sweat break out across his skin.

For long moments they simply held each other as he gathered her away from the edge.

"You are the bravest woman I ever met," he whispered, his lips skimming her hair, his hands stroking over her back and shoulders.

She shook her head. "I was scared."

"So was I. I knew he wasn't gonna drag us back to Baltimore to look for the money. And I knew damn well I had to think of something before we got to the canyon."

She nodded against his shoulder.

"Are you all right?"

"Yes. Was that what you wanted me to do—make him think there were nasty critters in here?"

"Yeah, that's what I was thinking. If you could shake him up, I could take him."

She lifted her head. "Where did he come from? Did you know who he was?"

"Vincent Reese."

"Am I supposed to know that name?"

He shook his head. "No. He's another player in this damn game."

"How did you know him? It didn't look like you'd met."

"We didn't. I'd found out from my boss at the Peregrine Connection that he was operating in this area. Him and his buddy. They were stalking the Sedgwick gang, trying to move in on them when money was changing hands. I guess he double-crossed his partner. He must be the guy I didn't recognize back there with the rest of the dead men."

Hannah shuddered, then looked toward the chasm. "How deep is it down there?"

"I don't know. But it's got to be deeper than the spot where I went over the side."

Her head jerked up. "You fell down there? That's what happened to you?"

He gave her a rueful look. "I still don't remember much about it. All I have is an image of myself flying over the edge into the darkness. But that makes sense." He shoved a hand through his hair. "The best I can reconstruct it, I was probably in here guarding the money. Then the shooting started, and I hustled toward the entrance when I heard the gunfire. I must have slipped on the loose gravel. Or maybe the ledge gave way. All that makes sense, but I still don't remember how I got out."

Her arms tightened around him. "You were too tough to die here. Either you walked out or you drove."

"Yeah."

She brought his mind back to the present when she asked, "How did Reese find us here?"

"I assume he had a lookout in town, in case I came back. Maybe his contact was our friend Diego."

"Maybe we should get out of here in case somebody else shows up."

"Yeah. But we'd better go back for our weapons."

He noted with amusement that she hadn't even been thinking about that. Taking her hand, he began leading her along the ledge, back the way they'd come, a much different journey than the first time. Now that Reese wasn't behind them, he felt as if a million-pound weight had been lifted off his shoulders.

"It's all over," she said with a sigh of relief as she forged ahead toward the end of the tunnel where they'd entered earlier.

He hated to shatter her feeling of safety, but there were still too many loose ends dangling. "Not yet."

Her fingers tightened on his. "You mean we're still in danger from Sedgwick's gang?"

"Sedgwick's men—and the Peregrine Connection."

"I understand about Sedgwick, but why would the Peregrine Connection come after you? You work for them."

"Either they think I'm dead, or they think I took off with a million dollars that doesn't belong to me."

"They know you're honest!"

"They know I *was* honest. I've got to tell them what happened here. Reese said he had a truck parked at the other end of the cave. We'll take it and get back to civilization. Not Pritchard. It's too hot for us there at the moment. Who knows how many spies have been paid to rat me out."

They retrieved their weapons and started back the way they'd come.

"Why was Sedgwick's gang meeting out here?" Hannah asked.

"To exchange money for drugs. I suggested the location, and they liked it because the cave has two entrances. I found it when I was a teenager prowling around in the desert when I needed to get away from my old man."

"You crossed into Mexico by yourself when you were a teenager? Wasn't that kind of dangerous?"

He shrugged.

"I guess you were a real asset to Sedgwick, knowing the country along the border."

"Yeah."

"Were there other meetings here?"

He nodded. "This was the third."

As he spoke, they reached the other end of the cave and stood facing a slitted opening in a rock wall. Luke paused, his hand on Hannah's arm.

"Wait," he ordered.

He cautiously emerged from the cave, blinking in the sunlight. Quickly he scouted the area, making sure that Reese had come alone. When he was satisfied, he started back for Hannah, a dull ache gripping the pit of his stomach because he knew what he had to do now.

Perhaps what he was feeling showed on his face because she drew in a little breath before asking, "What's wrong?"

"Nothing. I'm going to drop you off somewhere safe then get back to headquarters before they catch up with me."

"No!"

"I have to go back. Otherwise I'll be a fugitive for the rest of my life."

"I understand that part. I'm saying you're not dropping me off somewhere."

"You've done the job I hired you to do," he said in a flat voice. "Despite the fact that every step of the way I put you in danger. Now it's time for you to get out of the line of fire."

"You're saying that all you've wanted from me was help

getting your memory back?" she asked carefully. "And now that you have it, you don't need me anymore."

"Yes," he answered, because that was the only answer he could give her.

HANNAH LOOKED AWAY, unwilling to let him see the pain on her face. If that was the way he wanted things, she wasn't going to make a fool of herself by protesting.

Her throat burning, she followed him around a rock outcropping and toward a green SUV.

Out of habit, her eyes scanned the stark desert landscape. But her mind wasn't on the survey of her surroundings. She was thinking what a fool she'd been to assume her relationship with Luke was going to last, a fool to invest so much in a fantasy. He'd hired her to do a job. He'd been attracted to her. And when she'd thrown herself at him, he'd finally accepted what she was offering.

End of story.

No. Don't let him dictate the terms of surrender to you, she ordered herself. She'd walked into this relationship with her eyes wide open. Well, almost wide open. She'd come to understand the risks. And now just because he was acting the way he'd grown accustomed to acting—distancing himself— she wasn't going to cave.

She understood why he was doing it. It was partly because he felt guilty, and partly because he was scared. Scared to take the risk of reaching for what he wanted.

But she wouldn't simply let him walk away from her. She was going to fight for what they both wanted. And if she lost, she was going down swinging.

They climbed silently into the truck, and she was relieved to see the keys dangling from the ignition. When the air-conditioning kicked in, the chilled air sent a wave of shivers over her skin.

She slid Luke a look, but he was staring intently at the track ahead, which was hardly more than a place where two parallel lines left a series of tire marks.

"Are we going back the way we came?" she asked.

She saw him relax a notch. Probably he'd thought she was going to put up a fight. But she knew damn well that this wasn't the right time or the right place.

He pointed off to the left. "If I head this way, I can join up with the road in a couple of miles."

As they passed the canyon where she'd first seen the paintings on the wall, she longed to tell him what was in her heart. But again she made the decision to keep her own counsel, since he needed to focus on keeping them out of danger. So she sat beside him in silence, pretending she was going along with his fool decision.

She tensed as they approached the hill where the brakes had failed. But this time they were going the other way—in a well-tuned pickup, and there were no problems.

Then came the long stretch down toward the Rio Grande. They crossed the floodplain with its thick green vegetation, then came to the place where they'd forded.

The spot looked the same as it had the day before—an unofficial border crossing between Mexico and the U.S.

Hannah glanced at Luke. He was sitting with his hands wrapped around the wheel.

"What?" she asked.

"I don't know. It feels…" He let the sentence trail off.

"Wrong," she finished for him. "Can we cross somewhere else?"

He looked consideringly at the flowing water. "This is the only place around here where it's shallow enough."

As he started across, she felt like a thousand insects were crawling over her skin, buzzing in her brain. The reaction didn't make sense, she told herself. They were crossing to safety, to the U.S. side.

Still, her fingers dug into the edge of the seat as they splashed through the silty water.

They had reached the other bank and pulled onto the rock-strewn ground when suddenly the river cane around them shook and men poured onto the open area beside the river. Men dressed in the stark green uniforms of the border patrol.

"Luke Pritchard, halt," a voice sounded over a bullhorn. "Drop your weapon and come out with your hands up. You're under arrest."

CHAPTER SIXTEEN

Cursing loudly, Luke slammed on the brakes. Throwing the truck into Reverse, he sped back the way he'd come, the vehicle jouncing as if it were in an earthquake.

Bullets hit the front fenders, the tires, the hood. The engine sputtered. But he'd built up enough momentum to carry them backward across the river, then around a stand of mesquite trees.

"Out of the truck," he shouted, unbuckling his seat belt before the vehicle came to a halt. When he opened the door, he was overwhelmed by the smell of gasoline.

On the other side of the truck, Hannah stood coughing. But she didn't move.

"Come on!" he urged.

"Wait!" Ducking back inside, she reached for the pack of matches on the dashboard.

Keeping the truck between himself and the river, he charged around her side of the vehicle and grabbed her arm, trying to pull her toward a stand of mesquite trees.

But she dug in her heels. "No. Let me try this trick Matt Forester told me about."

"Who the hell is Matt Forester?"

"He works for Randolph Security. Like my friend Jed," she said as she struck one match and then another. "Get ready to run like hell," she added as she tossed them into the pool of liquid gathering under the truck.

He swore in admiration as the flames sprang to life. Together they plunged into the underbrush, putting as much distance as they could between themselves and the burning truck.

Even as he ran, he braced for the shock wave of an explosion. It came as a great rolling boom that shook the ground behind them.

"Smart idea. Maybe they'll think we went up in smoke," he breathed as he heard frantic shouts from the other side of the river.

Together they trotted westward, keeping a screen of river cane and mesquite between themselves and the water.

"The border patrol," Luke said. "That's all I need."

"It's not the border patrol," she answered.

His head whipped toward her. "What?"

"They've got the uniforms, but they're not lawmen," she repeated, then dragged in several breaths and let them out in a rush before rendering her professional opinion. "Well, maybe a bunch of green recruits who can't follow orders. I mean, they should have had this whole thing planned and rehearsed. But look at the way they jumped the gun when they came at the truck. They should have waited to block our escape exit. If they're trained law enforcement officers, they're pretty sorry. They came off more like a bunch of crooks with rudimentary instructions." She paused for breath, then plowed on. "And what about the mix of weapons? I'm pretty sure they weren't all standard issue."

He cocked his head to one side as he considered her assessment. "Yeah," he finally muttered. "I guess I was too busy getting the hell out of there to pick up on the details."

"So if they're not the border patrol, who are they?" she asked.

"Sedgwick's men, maybe. Nobody I recognize, though. Or somebody else who knows I came back to the area."

"Somebody with a lot of money, you mean. Enough to outfit a whole fake platoon."

"The uniforms could be stolen."

Before she could answer, the bullhorn sounded again. "Luke Pritchard, come out with your hands up."

"I'm dead. Blown up in the truck explosion," he muttered as they put more distance between themselves and the spot where they'd been ambushed.

"Where are we going?" Hannah asked.

"Where they won't expect us to go."

He kept up the pace, moving in a westward direction along the river, but far enough from the water so they wouldn't be spotted by anyone scanning the bank.

Finally, after he judged they'd put enough distance between themselves and the attack force, he made his way down to the water, staying behind a screen of low-growing plants.

Hannah followed. The river was perhaps thirty feet wide, and deeper than where the truck had forded. "We're going to the other side?" she asked.

"Right. Unfortunately, we'll be sitting ducks for a few minutes," he answered. Lord, he'd almost gotten her to safety. Now everything had blown up in his face again. Literally. But he kept his voice even as he said, "They're a lot less likely to look for us over there. And the farther we get from the river, the safer we'll be."

Hannah sat down in the sand to remove her boots and socks. Tying the laces securely together, she slung the boots over her shoulder.

"Do you think the water's up to my waist?"

"No," he answered, pulling off his own footwear. His didn't have laces, so he tucked them under his arm.

Removing her gun from the waistband of her jeans, she took a step toward the water and waded in. Just like that. Because she trusted him to get her out of this mess.

As she struggled to get her balance on the slippery rocks, he grabbed her hand to steady her.

He had been right in his assessment. He felt like a sitting duck as he waded with her toward the middle of the river. It rose to his knees, then seemed to level off as they made their way across the open space between the two banks.

It was hard to keep from making a headlong dash across the open expanse of water. But that would create noise as the water splashed around them. So he held tight to Hannah with one hand and to his gun with the other and moved at a slow but steady pace.

The bank drew closer with every step, and he was starting to believe they were actually going to make it, when a noise from above made her freeze.

Helicopters. Four of them, flying in formation, coming from the northeast. And there was no way in hell they couldn't have seen her and Luke in the water.

A curse erupted from his mouth. Tugging on Hannah's hand, he pulled her through the last few feet of water and onto dry land. They threw themselves into a stand of reeds.

He expected at least one of the choppers to circle their location. Instead, as he watched from their hiding place, all four machines proceeded down the river and around the bend.

He pulled on his boots and socks. Hannah did the same, just as the noise of gunfire erupted from around the bend in the river.

The guys in the helicopters were shooting at the fake border patrol. And the men on the ground were shooting back.

"What's going on?" Hannah asked, shouting above the din. "Who are they?"

"Don't know. Maybe the real border patrol."

"Why didn't they come after us?"

"Maybe they think we're small potatoes. Or they figure they can scoop us up when they finish with the Sedgwick gang. Come on."

He could see she wanted to protest. If the U.S. government had come swooping in, then maybe they were finally safe. The trouble was, he didn't know for sure it was the good guys up there—or whether they thought he and Hannah were on their side. So he clamped his hand on hers, leading her away from the sound of battle.

He was moving fast. Keeping up with him had her breath coming in gasps. He saw her press her hand against her side, doggedly trying to keep up. But he suspected she had a pretty bad stitch in her side and that she was at the end of her strength.

They broke from the cover of some trees. Ahead of her to the right he saw a cluster of old adobe buildings. A barn, a house, various sheds.

It looked like the ruins of a ranch.

He turned toward Hannah, looking critically at her flushed face, then back to the ranch. Changing direction, he headed toward the house. The door and roof were missing. The windows gaped. And there were probably snakes and scorpions.

But at the moment it looked as if Hannah didn't care about nasty critters as she followed him through the empty doorway. At the end of her strength, she wavered and would have toppled over if he hadn't gently caught her and leaned her against the wall. Shoulders pressed to the solid surface, she stood there panting, too tired to swipe at the trails of perspiration sliding down her face.

He wanted to reach for her, but he knew he didn't have the right. He'd done this to her. He'd gotten her into this mess. And now there was only one way to get her out.

THE RUINED HOUSE felt like a refuge, but Hannah knew in her heart that she was only conjuring up a false sense of security. Either the good guys or the bad guys would zero in on the buildings as soon as they broke away from the battle. If there were any good guys.

Luke must have drawn the same conclusion because when she looked up, he was checking his ammunition.

"Are we going to fight it out?"

"No." He turned toward her and took her by the shoulders. "You're going to rest here until you can go on."

"Until *we* can go on," she corrected.

He shook his head. "I'm staying to hold them off, darlin'. Your best chance is to get out of the area as fast as you can. If you can reach the highway, you can get help from a motorist. Then get the hell out of Texas. Go back to your friends at Randolph Security. They can protect you."

She waited until he had finished before shaking her head. "I'm not leaving you here. I didn't get a chance to say it, but I was never planning to let you dump me."

"Then you're a fool! They're after me, not you. Tell whoever wants to know that I've been dragging you along with me. That you finally escaped."

She looked at him in disbelief. "That's not an option. I'm not going to tell lies."

"You have to protect yourself."

Wavering on legs that looked as though they belonged to a rag doll, she lurched away from the wall, landing against him. Automatically, his arms came up to catch her, cradle her against his body.

"Luke…Lucas Somerville, you hired me to do a job and it's not finished."

"You're fired."

"Not good enough." Hannah's throat was unbearably tight, but she needed to tell him the rest of it—the important part. "I love you. I'm not leaving you in danger. If you can't deal with that, too bad."

His muttered curse made her stiffen. Then she relaxed as she felt the way he was cradling her in his arms.

"Luke, you've been trusting your instincts since you woke up in that Chicago hotel room," she murmured. "Just let yourself go a little further."

Maybe he would have said what she wanted to hear, she told herself, but the sound of the helicopter overhead interrupted the conversation. The choppers seemed to be flying in a wide circle around the ranch.

They both froze. Then Luke took her by the shoulders, pushing her to the door. "Go on. Run for it. I can hold them off." Moving toward the window, he stayed in the shadows while he craned his neck to the sky. "Damn. It looks like it's too late," he conceded.

The choppers were flying in a tighter and tighter formation, zeroing in on the ruined house.

As she watched, she could see them landing in a circle around their hiding place, cutting off all means of escape.

"How do they know we're here?" she gasped.

"I guess they've got sensors that can detect our body heat. Which means there wasn't any point in running."

"Too bad their sensors didn't pick up a herd of wild pigs. Or deer instead."

"I wish. I guess they can differentiate—by number of individuals and by body temperature."

Men ducked under the whirling blades as they climbed down from the helicopters, men with automatic weapons.

Her blood froze—until she spotted a familiar face.

"Jed. It's Jed Prentiss!" she cried out, relief flooding through her. "We're safe. He won't let anything happen to us."

The expression on Luke's face told her he didn't share her feeling of confidence. He looked from her to Jed, then back again. When he began to speak, his voice was cold and hard as falling hailstones. "I guess your friends at Randolph just couldn't pass up the chance to get their hands on a million dollars after all."

"No, they're here to rescue us."

"Then why are they armed? Why are they making sure we don't get away?"

She had no answer for that, no answer when another man stepped forward and raised a bullhorn.

"Lucas Somerville, we know you're in the house. You and the woman with you, Hannah Dawson. Drop your weapons and come out with your hands up."

The hairs on the back of Hannah's neck prickled. "Did I hear that right?"

He gave a bitter laugh. "You should have gotten out while the getting was good. It looks like whoever's out there is planning to take me down. Which leaves you in a rather awkward position—unless you're working with them."

"Luke, I'm not part of some damn conspiracy against you," she said, trying to understand what had gone so terribly wrong in the space of seconds. No, not in the space of seconds, she amended. Even if she didn't understand what was motivating the men outside, she understood where Lucas Somerville was coming from. He was falling back on old habits that he used to protect himself. Childhood habits, she reminded herself. And he was doomed to reenact the past, even though he'd denied that had anything to do with his motivation.

"Luke," she said quietly. "I would never hurt you. Never betray you. I love you."

His face was stony, and she knew he didn't believe her, would never believe her.

"Let me help you. Help us both," she pleaded.

"How?"

Before she could answer, the bullhorn sounded again. "Lucas Somerville, put down your weapons and surrender."

The voice was brusque, tense. To Hannah's ears, it sounded as though whoever was running the show had very little patience. She wanted to call out to Jed, ask him what was going on. But she could only assume he'd been given orders not to interfere.

Afraid they were out of time, she made a unilateral decision. Lifting her voice, she called to the men outside. "This is private investigator Hannah Dawson, formerly of the Baltimore City Police Department. I have Lucas Somerville in custody. I have disarmed him. I will bring him out peaceably if you lower your weapons."

There was dead silence outside, dead silence inside the ruined house. Then Luke spun her around to face him, his dark eyes smoldering with deeply ingrained emotions she could read all too well. "What the hell are you doing? Turning me over to them?"

"I'm taking our best chance to get out of here in one piece. If they see you come out with your hands up and me behind you with a gun, there won't be any trouble."

"You're either loco or—" His jaw tightened. Between clenched teeth he said, "I'm not going out unarmed, with my hands up like a damn criminal. How do you know it's not a trap, that they won't shoot us both?"

"Because Jed's there. He won't shoot me or you."

"You'd bet your life on that?"

"Yes."

"And you expect me to trust you now?"

"Yes," she said simply, holding her breath as she waited for his answer.

He stood staring at her, not speaking, and she tried to give him more reason to trust her, trust the odds.

"That's not Sedgwick's gang who's got us surrounded. It's a well-disciplined federal force."

He gave a harsh laugh. "Did you see the news clips on Waco or Ruby Ridge? Some hot dog out there could be looking for an excuse to fire. If you step outside armed, you could give them that excuse."

She opened her mouth to speak then closed it again. When she'd made her hasty declaration, she hadn't been thinking in those terms. She'd been thinking of the men she knew and trusted in law enforcement. Now she understood Luke's logic. "Okay, then I'll put my hands up, too," she said.

Seconds ticked by; each one felt like a year of her life. Finally he said, "The longer we stay here, the more excuse we give them to rush us. There's a lot of them out there. They know they can take us. But going out is a risk, too. If you're bound and determined to give yourself up, I'll do it with you. What do I have to lose besides my life?"

Her fingers closed around his arm. "You're not going to lose anything," she breathed. But even as she gave him that assurance, she felt a trickle of sweat slide down her neck.

"We'd better do it," she said. "Go to Jed. He'll know what to do."

Looking like a man facing a firing squad, Luke carefully set down his gun and raised his hands.

"Lucas Somerville and I are coming out," she shouted. "We are both unarmed. I repeat, we are both unarmed. Hold your fire. We're coming out." She turned to Luke. "I'll go first."

"No!" He stepped in front of her, blocking the doorway, his hands in the air.

Black spots gathered in her field of vision. Unconsciously braced for the sound of gunfire, she followed him into the late-afternoon sunshine, her own hands raised to shoulder level. Somewhere a two-way radio crackled, and a man's voice came over the speaker, too far away for her to make out what he was saying. The ring of armed men surrounding them danced in her vision.

She wanted to grab Luke's arm and pull him back inside. Instead, she walked, matching her pace to his slow stride. Faces swam in and out of focus. She picked out Jed Prentiss, locked on to him as Luke walked in her friend's direction.

Then from the side of the ring, a figure pushed through the line of men.

"He's got a gun," someone shouted.

Who? Who had a gun?

She saw sunlight flash on metal. Saw the weapon.

Even as the gun discharged, Luke was pushing her down, throwing himself on top of her.

CHAPTER SEVENTEEN

Hannah felt a bullet hit the ground inches from her head. Then another shot sounded, and she felt Luke's body jump.

"No!" she cried out, pulling him to her, struggling to reverse their positions so that she was the one on top. But he kept her pinned to the ground.

She could see nothing, only hear the sounds of chaos around her. Men shouting. Someone scuffling.

Then two more shots. Only, the bullets were nowhere near her.

"Luke." The blood draining from her head as she saw his white face. "Where were you hit?"

"It's nothing," he said between clenched teeth.

"Where?"

"My arm." He pushed himself up, looking at the frozen faces, the drawn guns around them.

Belatedly she remembered where she was and why they were there.

"Put your weapons away," someone ordered.

The agents around them complied as two men strode forward. One was young and had a medical kit. He knelt beside Luke. The other was older and looked as if he was in authority.

Ignoring him, Hannah hovered over Luke, who grimaced as the medic ripped off his shirtsleeve.

"How is he?"

"It's not serious. The bullet went clean through. But I have to stop the bleeding."

"I'm fine!" Luke insisted.

"Clear the area. I want the area cleared," the older man said.

She could see Jed among the crowd nearby. But when the man gave the order, armed men moved everybody back, including her friend. When the newcomer had obtained a measure of privacy, he touched her arm. "Come over here where we can talk."

She climbed to her feet, looked back to see that Luke was being taken care of and let the man lead her a short distance away.

"Miss Dawson, I'm Frank Dean. I represent the agency Lucas works for."

A helicopter engine almost drowned out his speech, and she let him usher her to the side of the ranch house where the noise wasn't so great.

"The Peregrine Connection?" she asked when they could finally speak again.

He nodded.

"Well, you'd better listen to what I have to say. The reason Luke didn't contact you was that he lost his memory. He didn't know who he was, and he hired me to help him find out—and help him figure out why he ended up with a suitcase full of money. We've been chased all over Baltimore, all over southwest Texas. And now you're trying to kill him."

"No. We're not trying to kill him," the man answered. He paused for a second before going on. "That was somebody from the Sedgwick gang who must have followed you from the river. I guess he figured that if you weren't going to turn the money over, nobody was going to get it."

That explanation didn't quite ring true. "He wasn't dressed like the border patrol. They were all in green uniforms."

The man's eyes bored into hers. "The official explanation is that he was working with the Sedgwick gang. I suggest that you accept it."

Hannah felt a shiver go up her spine. *The official explanation.* Just what the hell had happened here this afternoon? She would find out, but she understood that it wouldn't be now.

"Jed Prentiss apprised us of the situation last night. Everything's under control now. We understand that Lucas would have returned to headquarters if he'd been able."

She looked back to the spot where Luke had been lying. He was gone! Seconds later, a helicopter took off.

Savagely, she turned back toward Dean. "What have you done with Luke? Why were you treating this like a tactical arrest?"

"His wound needs attention. And we have to debrief him."

She repeated the last question, the one he'd sidestepped. "Answer me, damn you! Why did you come here with an armed force?"

"Because we didn't know what we were going to find when we got here. Because even after Jed's assurances there was some question about his loyalty. The only way we could keep him out of danger was to make sure the situation was under strict control."

Perhaps that made some kind of sense, Hannah conceded. If there were elements here who still thought Luke had run away with a million dollars, they would want assurances that he couldn't make any trouble. A shiver went through her. "What would have happened if he hadn't agreed to come out with his hands up?"

"We were prepared to immobilize him," Dean answered,

but his expression told her that he wasn't prepared to answer any more of her questions.

Anger bubbled inside her. It took all her restraint to keep from popping him on the chin. Dean must have read her savage expression because he took a step back.

"I want to be with Luke."

"You will be," he said soothingly. "He'll be fine. You can come out on the next chopper."

SIX HOURS LATER, after changing transportation at a military base, she arrived in Berryville, Virginia, at a charming old mansion that turned out to be the headquarters of the Peregrine Connection. That was about all anyone would tell her, besides the fact that Luke was fine.

Then they'd showed her to a suite of rooms furnished with what looked like priceless antiques. When the door had locked behind her, she'd kicked it several times in frustration.

Running her hand through her tangled hair, she realized she must look as if she'd just staggered out of the desert. So she accepted the Peregrine Connection's hospitality and repaired to the bathroom, where she took a shower, then changed into the clean clothing they gave her, a pair of slacks and a pretty turquoise blouse that looked like something she might have chosen for herself.

Lying down on the bed fully dressed, she knew there was no chance of sleeping. Her mind kept circling back to the scene at the ruined ranch. To Dean and what he'd told her. Had Luke's boss really believed he was innocent? Was he hedging his bets with the tactical arrest? And who was the shooter who had started firing at them?

It was two in the morning when she finally heard the door

lock click. Springing off the bed, she prepared to assault whoever came through the door.

But she lowered her hands when Jed Prentiss walked in. "Jed, what are you doing here? What's going on? Nobody will tell me anything!"

"I'm here because I used to be a Peregrine agent before I came to work for Randolph Security. I was asked to give you some information."

"Thank God. How is Luke?"

"He's in excellent shape, considering."

"I want to see him."

"Soon."

Her eyes narrowed. "Whose side are you on, Jed?"

"Yours."

Sighing, she switched tactics. "Then tell me who ordered the tactical arrest. And who tried to kill us. I know damn well it wasn't somebody from Sedgwick's gang."

"Where does that assessment come from?"

"Common sense."

He sighed. "I'm authorized to tell you what happened, provided the information goes no further than this room."

She might have let that make her angry, except she wasn't going to get distracted from the main subject.

"Who authorized the operation and who was the shooter?" she asked firmly.

"Luke's boss, Addison Jennings, authorized the operation. It was the only way out of a bad situation. He was walking a tightrope, trying to bring Luke in when certain people wouldn't believe he was still loyal to the Peregrine Connection."

"It looks like those certain people didn't agree with Jennings's decision."

"The shooter was a loose cannon—a government operative with misguided loyalties," he said.

"Who ordered the hit?"

"Everything worked out all right so let's just leave it at that."

She didn't want to leave it at that, but she suspected that was all she was going to get from Jed.

"Luke's in no danger from the government now?" she pressed.

"That's right."

"What guarantee do I have of that?"

"Jennings is taking care of the individual responsible. The case is closed."

"But—"

"Do you want to stand here arguing with me or do you want to go see your guy?"

"I want to see him." She raised her face to Jed and swallowed. "I have the feeling Luke's coming through this has a lot to do with you."

He shrugged.

She came to him and gave him a quick, heartfelt hug. "Jed, thank you. Thank you for everything."

"I'm glad things worked out. Now go on. He's down the hall. Third door on the right."

She needed no further invitation. Flying down the corridor, she flung open the door Jed had indicated and found Luke wearing a track across the Oriental rug. His left arm was in a sling, under an unbuttoned shirt that hung loosely over his left shoulder. Otherwise, he looked as if he was in pretty good shape.

She didn't know what she intended to say until words tumbled out of her mouth. "I want you to understand that whoever may have left you in the past—or hurt you—wasn't me. I'm not going to do that. If you want me to leave, you'll have to send me away."

The look of wonder and relief on his face nearly shattered her.

"You want to be with me, even after the way I bad-mouthed you back at that ranch house?"

"Yes." She wanted to leap forward and throw her arms around him, but she was afraid she'd hurt him. So she stepped close to him and clasped his good hand as she laid her head on his shoulder. "What you said under stress doesn't matter," she whispered, pushing the shirt aside with her cheek and brushing her lips against his collarbone. "What matters was you stepped out the door first knowing it might all go bad. Then when somebody started shooting at us, you threw me to the ground and shielded me with your body. I think that makes it kind of hard to hide how you feel. But you can go on trying if you like."

"Darlin', I couldn't hide my feelings back in the Last Chance Bar. I just got…scared for a while." He swallowed. "Scared to let you find out how much I needed you. I love you. I reckon it's time to stop fighting it."

She could hardly believe what she'd heard. "You love me?"

"Oh, yeah." He punctuated the declaration with a kiss that left her breathless.

When he lifted his head, his expression was fierce. "Lock the door."

Her head was suddenly spinning, but she managed that simple task. When she turned back to him, she found he was grinning at her, looking happier and more relaxed than she'd ever seen him.

Lifting one finger, she gently touched the sexy dimples on his cheeks. Then she touched them with her lips.

She felt him fumbling with the buttons on her shirt and realized he was having trouble working them with one hand.

"Dang," he muttered. "I'd like to toss this damn sling."

"Not to worry." Smiling mischievously at him, she undid her shirt, flung it away, then got rid of her bra.

He sucked in a quick breath, lifting his hand to cup her breast. She leaned into his touch, her own breath catching as she pushed the open shirt off his shoulders and started working on his belt buckle.

By the time she had them both naked, except for the sling, they were breathing hard and swaying dangerously on their feet.

"I think we'd better lie down," he whispered.

She scooted onto the bed, then held out her arms to him, and he came down beside her, scowling at the injured arm.

"The downside of chivalry," he muttered.

"There's an upside, too," she answered in a silky voice. Kneeling beside him, she slid her lips over his chest, his belly, and lower, her own arousal building to fever pitch as she saw the effect she was having on him.

"Hannah, darlin'. Please," he gasped, his hand gripping her hip. "Don't make me wait any longer."

She was in complete agreement. With a smile, she straddled him and brought him inside of her. As she gazed down at him, the look of love on his face took her breath away.

He loved her! She knew it with a certainty that brought a low moan to her throat. And he wasn't afraid to let her see the naked emotion on his face.

"Oh, Luke," she whispered.

The fingers of his good hand laced with hers, clasping her tightly as she began to move, her pleasure spiraling quickly upward, her eyes misting as she saw her joy mirrored on his face.

Control slipped away. Her movements became wild,

frantic, as the mounting pleasure carried her toward release. She felt his body tense, heard his shout of pleasure, just before the towering climax rolled over her.

Spent, she sagged against him, and he cradled her with his good arm. She was too tired to do more than drift.

But the tone of his voice snapped her to full alertness. "Pleasure first. Now business."

She lifted her head. "What business?"

"Do you want to know who ran you out of the ranch yard and ambushed us at the adobe?"

"Yes."

"Men from town, apparently, who didn't like a local boy being in the middle of a drug-smuggling operation. The guy who went after you with the pickup was warning us away. Then when Diego found out I hadn't given up on going into the desert, they set up the ambush."

"And one of them was willing to kill the other? That's pretty…desperate."

"They *were* desperate. They knew if their plan got back to Sedgwick, he'd come take revenge on the whole town. So they'd made a suicide pact."

She sucked in a shuddering breath, thinking of the man who had died. Then her mind bounced back to the ruthless mob leader. "What happened to Sedgwick?"

"I wish to hell I knew. The Peregrine Connection raided his hideout at the same time they came to rescue us. He got away. But one of his key men was found dead—a bastard named Chad Crosby." He cleared his throat. "So that's one reason we're gonna have to stay out of circulation for a while. Until we know Sedgwick's in custody, that's the only way we can stay safe."

"One reason?" she asked. "What's the other?"

"The situation in Baltimore."

"Meaning?" she asked cautiously.

"Well, for starters, Jennings told me why my subconscious mind took me to Baltimore. I knew the drugs that Sedgwick is smuggling across the border are ending up there. So I must have remembered that connection on some level."

She nodded.

"That makes it dangerous for me to go back," he continued. "But it's just as dangerous for you. You can keep arguing that the attack on you after you left the Last Chance Bar was random, but I think differently. I think it was someone trying to avenge Sean Naylor."

She had been wondering about that, too, after Ron Wexler's death. But she'd been afraid to admit it, even to herself. "Who?"

"Sean's father."

"How did you come to that conclusion?"

"I've had your friends check it out. That police detective, Cal Rollins. And that other P.I. in your office, Sam Lassiter. I figured that since they found out I'm not working for the mob, I might as well take advantage of their help."

"You've been busy," she commented wryly.

"The senior Naylor's been mouthing off all over town. He's had a lot to say about police bungling. He wanted everyone to know that Sean was simply an innocent bystander gunned down by the department. Now he's gone underground. Until he turns up, I want you where I know you're safe."

He looked as if he was prepared for an argument. But Hannah wasn't stupid. She'd found the man with whom she wanted to spend the rest of her life, and she wasn't going to spoil it by getting killed, just to prove she hadn't lost her nerve. She'd already proved everything she needed to prove in the desert.

"All right," she said quietly.

"All right. Just like that?"

She stroked her fingers lightly across his chest, loving the feel of the curly hairs against her fingers. "Well, there are a couple of conditions."

His expression turned wary again. "Like what?"

"What kind of long-term commitments were you thinking of?"

He looked thunderstruck, as though he hadn't thought much beyond the next few days. But he recovered quickly. "Would you...would you..." He cleared his throat. "Would you consider gettin' hitched? I mean, if I got out of the spy business. I know it's too dangerous for a married man."

It wasn't exactly the most romantic proposal she could imagine, but she heard the love shimmering below the words and saw the fear in his eyes. He looked like a man standing at the edge of the Grand Canyon, afraid someone was going to push him off.

Turning toward him, Hannah brushed her lips against his. "I was hoping you'd work up the nerve to ask."

He laughed, tension easing out of him. "I thought you might think getting hitched to me was too much of a risk."

"I told you. I love you. I'm never planning to walk away from you. Never."

He cuddled her close, stroked his lips against her cheek. But when he spoke, his voice was serious. "I haven't thought much about what I'm going to do. I don't know any other jobs—besides ranching, and my dad killed my taste for that." She guessed that for the first time in a long while he didn't feel the pain in his gut at the thought of his past. "Although,

I figure I don't have to worry about an income right away. Addison's letting me keep the million. Or what's left of it." He couldn't stop the smile that curved his lips. "Said I deserved it, after what I went through."

"He's right." She reached to stroke his lips. "And when you're ready, I think that with your background, if you tried Randolph Security, they'd be glad to have you."

"You reckon?"

"Yes."

"I was afraid this was going to be hard. It's easier than I thought," he said with a look of wonder.

"Because we have each other. Because if you love someone, you do what it takes to make a good life together. I know it's scary for you to believe in that, but I'll prove it to you every day of our lives."

"I knew I was making the right decision when I hired you," he whispered, the raspy quality of his voice melting her heart. "Even if I couldn't admit to myself that I wanted a lot more than a private detective. I guess you know that I never thought much about the future. I was always living in the present, living for my job—because that was the only place where I felt comfortable. But you've made me understand there's so much more."

She ducked her head to hide the tears blurring her vision, overwhelmed that he had come so far in such a short time. "I'm glad you figured it out," she murmured, knowing that the years ahead with this man would bring her joy beyond imagining.

* * * * *

Fall in Love with...

MEN
in UNIFORM

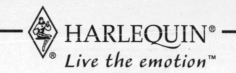

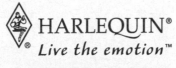

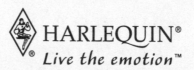

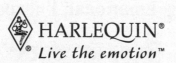

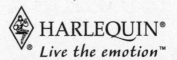

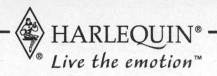